To Whom the Heart Decided to Love

Fr. Lawrence Edward Tucker, SOLT

⊕ENROUTE
Make the time

En Route Books and Media, LLC
5705 Rhodes Avenue
St. Louis, MO 63109

Cover credit: TJ Burdick

Library of Congress Control Number: 2018941134

ISBN-13: 978-0-9998814-6-0
ISBN-10: 0-9998814-6-9

DEDICATION

This book is dedicated to my mother.

CHAPTER ONE

My dear friend, I am going to share my journey through life with you. Perhaps you will enjoy it. Maybe it will help you in some way. An individual does not lose the desire or the capacity to share simply because that person is living in Heaven. The fact of the matter is . . . it's just the opposite; it's pure joy for me to share my life with you! Now that I'm here in Heaven, you could say that sharing is who I am; I have been missioned, as it were, to whom the heart decided to love.

Heaven is indeed as wonderful as we were told it would be. In fact, it's so beautiful I really can't describe it. As we read in 1 Corinthians, 2:9: "Eye has not seen, ear has not heard . . . nor has it ever dawned upon the mind of man . . that which God has prepared for those who love him!" Suffice to say . . . we were made for Heaven; and not to arrive here would be the greatest catastrophe that could ever befall a human person. Such a thought is practically unthinkable . . . especially to those of us who are already here enjoying the eternal communion of life and love that we share with God and one another.

The key word here is SHARE . . . because Christian life is essentially about sharing. Creation itself is nothing less than a wondrous act of sharing that manifests the goodness and beauty of our Father's eternal love. And when his children found themselves imprisoned in their own self-inflicted isolation, he shared his son with them so they could be free to live in communion once again. A person living in communion with Jesus receives not only the capacity to share . . . but the capacity to share one's very self! This particular gift is a marvel of inestimable value!

My name is Benjamin Lake. I was not always a person who was interested in sharing. Truth be told, I was about as interested in sharing as a thief is interested in getting caught! The word sharing was barely even present in my vocabulary. The only time I used it was when I was trying to convince someone else to share something of value with me. You see, Benjamin Lake was, by anyone's assessment, a very wealthy man . . . and his every thought, word, and deed was focused on staying that way.

The mere thought of losing my status as a multi-billionaire was enough to bring upon me such a degree of angst that I would practically cease functioning . . . until my mind returned to happier thoughts; such as the luxurious interior of my newest yacht. Based on this "inside information," you might get the impression that I did not live in the real world. I did live in the real world. It's just that the real world I lived in was my own . . . I shared it with no one.

I did nothing at all to earn my position as one of the wealthiest people in the world. I was, as the saying goes, "born with a silver spoon in my mouth." That being said, I was certainly diligent in doing whatever was necessary to keep that silver spoon in its rightful place! I luxuriated in every hedonistic minute of my pampered existence to such a degree that, if you had asked me if I was enjoying life, I probably would have responded that I was so comfortable it seemed as though life was enjoying me!

My net worth at any given moment was around 75 billion dollars. Not bad for a 30-year-old man who did nothing with his life other than earn a PhD in Greek and Latin Literature (Classical Philology) from Harvard University. When I wasn't counting my money you might find me reading Herodotus (a Greek historian) in the original Greek. I was fond of quoting him to people who criticized my superficial and indulgent lifestyle: "If a man insisted on being serious and never allowed himself a bit of fun and relaxation, he would go mad or become unstable without knowing it."

Of course, I was already, at least in the spiritual sense, "mad and unstable" . . . I simply didn't know it. Not knowing the truth about my own interior life was inevitable since I surrounded myself with people who were just as lost as I was. Talk about the "blind leading the blind;" if the world had indeed been flat, my friends and I would have walked off the edge of it a long time ago. And what's worse, we would have considered the event to be far less disastrous than the horrifying prospect of losing our wealth!

Wealth is a funny thing; do we have it . . . or does it have us? I inherited all of my wealth from my father, Thomas Lake. My father's fortune was based on various minerals he owned, such as petroleum, gas, gold, and silver. The capital generated by these valuable minerals afforded him the opportunity to create one of the most lucrative hedge funds Wall Street had ever seen. Not one to rest on his laurels, my father went on to form an innovative, privately-owned bank based in Manhattan, NYC. He named the bank Praetergressus Bank (Latin for

Advance Beyond Bank) . . . because he said most banks spend too much time and energy looking back to see how things were done in the past and not enough time looking forward to see where the world is going. His bank would be the first to recognize and take advantage of all the golden opportunities that were likely to surface as the global economy unfolded . . . even if it meant that the traditional concept of what a bank is and does would have to morph and develop accordingly.

Unfortunately, although my father was something of a visionary in the world of finance and business, when it came to flying . . . he was as blind as a bat! One day, while dropping down low to survey one of his many properties, his small plane's wing clipped the edge of a cellphone tower and he and my dear mother, Anne Sheldon Lake, died due to injuries suffered in the tragic crash that followed.

To say I was devastated by the sudden loss of my parents doesn't even begin to express accurately the sense of emptiness and confusion that was thrust upon me. Without doubt, I was the third victim of that plane crash; a part of me deep inside died that day . . . and was just as dead as my mother and father. I was an only child and therefore I had in essence lost my entire family. Although I had become accustomed to not having any brothers or sisters, the loss of the closest relatives I did have was a veritable knock-out punch.

Of course, as a child, the absence of siblings did have its benefits . . . and this fact was not lost on me. Growing up, I regaled in the attention that was lavished upon me by my parents . . . and I bristled when they showed even the least bit of attention to any of my cousins. Being born into magnificent wealth is one thing. But being raised in a situation where, due to the absence of siblings, one is not required to share any of the things that great wealth provides was, in retrospect, more of a curse than a blessing. Yes . . . I did have friends. And as Euripides, an ancient Greek dramatist, pointed out: "One loyal friend is worth ten thousand relatives." But I could not lay claim to one trustworthy friend; let alone a loyal one.

Both my parents were Catholic, so for the most part, I was raised a Catholic. We lived in a luxury, 4-bedroom apartment on 5th Avenue, NYC, and went to St. Patrick's Cathedral for Sunday mass. I can still hear my father calling me on Sunday mornings: "Benjamin . . . how are you doing? It's almost time for mass!" And I would respond: "I'm ready dad . . . can I sit next to you in Church?" All too often, I would have to endure his disappointing rejoinder: "I'm sorry, Benny, but I have an important business meeting and I have to leave town this morning. I'll be back in a couple of days and we'll go for a nice walk together in Central Park."

It's not that I didn't enjoy walking with my father in Central Park. I loved it! I could hardly wait until we reached the statue of Alice in Wonderland so I could climb all over it with the other children playing there. But when dad didn't go to Church with us, it practically neutralized the whole reason for going in the first place . . . which was to have communion with God and one another. Without realizing it, my father was teaching me something that, unfortunately, I ended up learning all too well . . . money is more important than God. But neither my father nor I ever learned the real lesson we so desperately needed to learn . . . "No man can serve two masters." (Matthew 6:24). One of the most beautiful things about Heaven is that everyone here loves God with their whole heart, their

Fr. Lawrence Edward Tucker, SOLT

whole soul, and their whole mind; no divided hearts in Heaven! Very often in life, the simplest things are the hardest to learn.

How I got over the loss of my parents, I don't really know. But I do know this . . . I did not turn to God; I turned to the world. Having attended the United Nations International School (UNIS) in Manhattan, NYC, for twelve years, and Harvard University in Cambridge, Massachusetts, for ten years, I did, quite literally, know the world! As the saying goes, I had "friends in high places;" not just in my own country . . . but all over the planet (thanks especially to my twelve years in UNIS).

I threw myself into the world the same way a pig carelessly throws itself about in the mud and slop of its pen. And it worked! I lost myself in a whirlwind of pointless trips around the globe, reckless spending, and such mindless, bacchanalian revelry that my cousin Geoffrey, who was next in line to inherit the Lake fortune, was beginning to think seriously about how he would handle things when I finally succeeded in killing myself.

St. Ignatius of Loyola said that one of the ways you can tell if you have made a wrong decision is if the decision causes feelings of spiritual "desolation;" that is, if the soul feels agitated by interior turmoil and is impulsively drawn to base and worldly things . . . while being beset by unusual temptations. Clearly, based on those criteria, the decision I made was wrong . . . very wrong! But my moral compass had by then been so eroded I was not fully alert to the destructive potential of this new direction. In fact, I'm not even sure I was aware of having consciously made any kind of a "decision." I moved so quickly and so instinctively into my escape mode that I was in "cognitive-override" and was careening down a dangerous path at breakneck speed . . . on automatic pilot!

I was running from myself. Life had become a tremendous burden, and I could not find the strength or the desire to carry it any longer. "Benjamin . . . you had better snap out of it!" yelled my cousin Geoff, "If you continue like this you will squander your inheritance . . . as did the prodigal son; only you don't have a father to return to!" But my cousin's concern was not sincere. The one thing he was sincerely concerned about was the fact that I was wasting what would be his inheritance should I die. So much for the warmth presumed to exist between blood relatives. When money takes the place of God in a family, then love, that priceless, heavenly treasure, is replaced by worldly greed.

CHAPTER TWO

How I arrived at my family's vacation home in *Costa del Sol, Spain,* I really can't say. My life at that time had become so chaotic and confused it was just a huge, all-encompassing blur! Here I was in a foreign country with no knowledge of how I got there or why I had gone there in the first place. Did I take the yacht . . . did I take the jet? Was I alone in the house or were others there with me? I wasn't sure, and, deep down . . . I really didn't care.

I stumbled out of my bedroom and down the stairs to the main floor of our beautiful home overlooking the marina. It was a glorious morning in *Costa del Sol* so I threw open the curtains to let in the sun which was only too happy to enter. The sunlight rushed in with such joyful exuberance that, for just a moment, thoroughly surprised and drenched in the warmth of that brilliant, celestial light . . . I felt something . . . something different; something I hadn't felt since my parent's death 6 months previous. For a split second . . . I felt human again!

I looked out the window in the direction of the marina to see if my 200 foot yacht, *AMIGO,* was there. It was not. I knew then that I had come to Spain in my jet . . . which meant that my pilot, Pancho Luna, would be staying at a nearby hotel waiting to hear from me regarding my travel plans. I determined to call him after breakfast, but first I needed to sit for a few minutes and reflect on what I had just experienced when I was bathed in that overwhelming flood of sunlight.

As I sat there on our magnificent, rustic couch made of rugged, Spanish leather from *Extremadura,* I realized something; my mental state was different . . . improved, as it were. For one thing, in the past six months I hadn't stopped for a single moment to reflect on anything. And there I was, sitting calmly and thinking about my life. It seemed odd, or I should say, it seemed altogether normal, and thoroughly human!

In the midst of my meditation, one feeling in particular, perhaps we can call it a spiritual intuition, arose within me and dominated my consciousness. That feeling was what is commonly referred to as . . . hope. Yes, I was experiencing hope!

As strange as it sounds, experiencing hope was something I had long since given up hope for! Yet, there I was . . . acting and feeling like a normal, "flesh and blood" human being who, for some wonderful, mysterious reason, had hope back in his life.

Pancho must have called the cook because I could hear her preparing breakfast in the kitchen: "Quisiere desayunar, Señor Lake?" (Would you like breakfast, Mr. Lake?) asked the cook. "Yes . . . Thank you, Ángela." I replied. "Mr. Lake . . . Pancho is waiting to hear from you." "Thank you, Ángela . . . I'll give him a call right now." As I made my way over to the other side of the room to make my call, the phone rang.

"Good morning, Mr. Lake, its Memphis. How is everything in Costa del Sol?" (Ms. Memphis Taylor was my executive secretary) . . . "All is well, Memphis . . . how are things back in New York?" "We're good here, Mr. Lake. I just wanted to check with you regarding your big meeting the day after tomorrow in San Cristobal de Las Casas, Chiapas, Mexico. Do you need anything from us here at head office?" Well . . . not only had I completely forgotten about the meeting, I had no recollection whatsoever regarding the reason for the meeting.

"Thank you, Memphis, yes . . . I seem to have misplaced my notes. I'm sure I have an outline of the meeting in my laptop, but in the meantime, could you give me a quick rundown on the meeting over the phone?" "Sure, Mr. Lake. You and Pancho have reservations to stay at the *HOTEL BO*, in San Cristobal from Monday to Friday. It's not the Waldorf Astoria, but it's a five-star hotel and you should be very comfortable there. Your first meeting is on Tuesday evening in *El Restaurante Lum* . . . the hotel restaurant. There will be two representatives of the Mexican government present at that dinner: Mr. Juan Ortiz, the Secretary of Finance, and Mr. Raul Ortega, the Secretary of the Environment.

On Wednesday morning, you will be given a tour of San Cristobal de Las Casas. Present at lunch that afternoon will be the Secretary of the Interior, Mr. Marcos Ruiz, the highest ranking member of the President's Cabinet. The other two Secretaries will also be present at that lunch. The luncheon on Wednesday will be the main business meeting. All the Cabinet members will return to Mexico on Wednesday evening. Thursday is a free day for you . . . rest, shop, do whatever you please. On Friday, Pancho will fly you back to New York; any questions?

"Eh . . . yes, Memphis, just one question; exactly what is it we will be discussing at those meetings?" "You're kidding, right Mr. Lake?" replied Memphis, in a jovial tone of voice, "Oh . . . no, I get it; you want to see just how much I know about the meeting! Ok . . . here goes: it's very simple . . . the Mexican government is considering the possibility of developing eco-tourism in the *Lacandon Jungle* . . . specifically, in the *Montes Azules Biosphere Reserve,* and they want to see if *Praetergressus Bank,* in other words, you . . . would be interested in investing in such a project."

"But here's the catch," Memphis continued, "*Praetergressus Bank* is not interested in ecotourism. What we want, or I should say, what our investors want, is petroleum development in the Lacandon. Remember . . . our biggest investors are oil and gas people mostly from Texas but from other parts of the country as well. And don't forget that Texas Senator, Anderson, who's putting a great deal of pressure on us to encourage drilling in the Biosphere Reserve. He said that oil from Mexico is what is enabling the USA to move away from purchasing oil from our enemies in the Middle East. And he added that, consequently, you would be something of a traitor to your country if you did not push the drilling agenda."

"Excellent, Memphis! You really are an extraordinary assistant . . . where would I be without you!" Homeless and living under a bridge was the short answer to that question!

"Hold on, Mr. Lake, I almost forgot . . . there's one more thing: the Mexican Secretary of Energy, Ricardo Villanueva, was not invited by the Mexican government to be present at these meetings. All things considered, that's understandable. But he's the one who is most important to us because we know he's the only Cabinet member in favor of drilling. We can presume that he stands to make a great deal of money if the *Montes Azules Biosphere Reserve* in the *Lacandon Jungle* is opened up for energy/petroleum development."

"That's why we arranged, at his request, a private meeting between the two of you on Wednesday evening; the other Secretaries know nothing about this meeting. The meeting will give both of you an opportunity to explore the various options regarding the oil agenda. You should know that the strongest opposition to the agenda is coming from the poor, indigenous people of that region who are vehemently against drilling. The environment-alists will also present a serious problem. The meeting will take place, fittingly enough, in *Restaurante El Secreto*, on Avenida 16 de Septiembre, #24, at 9:00 pm. Just tell the host your name, and you will be lead to a small, private dining area . . . any questions?"

"No, Memphis . . . thanks so much! Talk to you later. Ciao!" It all sounded great to me. There was some serious money to be made here if I could just work out some kind of an effective strategy with the Secretary of Energy, Ricardo Villanueva. Although I didn't have much experience as an executive in the business world, over the years I had watched and listened enough to my father to pick up on most of the basics. After sitting in on a number of business deals with my dad (occasionally, he would allow me to handle one on my own), he saw my potential and begged me to enroll in the Harvard Business School. But I had become fascinated with the ancient world and was determined to enter the Harvard program for Classical Studies.

Nevertheless, I had developed a taste for the "finer things," the finest of which was money! Making money, therefore, was more or less instinctive with me. The prospect of landing this deal in Chiapas was something that fell right into my "wheelhouse," as they say. When a sizable amount of cash was up for grabs, I could become extremely focused and motivated. Then, like the famous *Wolfman,* undergoing his transition from human to wolf, I would feel the greed rise up within me . . . as my humanity drained away.

Faith in God is a wonderful thing; but if we don't have it . . . what will save us from ourselves as we pass through the gauntlet of passions that assail us while we journey through life? My faith was weak to begin with. But when that plane carrying my parents crashed, the modicum of faith I had crashed with it. As I mentioned earlier, the loss hardened my heart and I became noticeably colder emotionally, which is really saying something . . . considering how I was never "Mr. Sensitivity" to begin with. I couldn't care less about the poor, the indigenous or the environment. My job was to make money. I didn't have the time or the energy for these other, petty considerations. That was someone else's job.

This was the mindset I would generally have when I was preparing to engage other businessmen in a struggle for the best possible deal. I didn't know why but I noticed that this time I wasn't slipping into my "dog-eat-dog" mode, as I had done so often in the past. I figured I was exhausted and lacked the energy needed to get psyched-up. In any case I was, relatively speaking, rather mellow as I prepared for my trip to Mexico.

I called Pancho and told him we would have to leave in the morning for Miami, and the following morning we would fly to San Cristobal.

CHAPTER THREE

"What a beautiful hotel, Mr. Lake! Have you ever stayed here before?" asked Pancho. "No, Pancho," I answered, "I've never had any reason to come to San Cristobal. But I agree with you; this place is very unique – super artistic! I'm exhausted and I'm sure you are as well. Tomorrow, I will rest up and prepare for the first meeting. Feel free to take any of the tours or use any of the services offered by the hotel. I probably won't see much of you during the week, but we will definitely meet up for breakfast at 9am, Friday morning. And then, after breakfast, off we go to New York City." "Sounds good, Mr. Lake," said Pancho, "¡Vaya con Dios!" Pancho was a Mexican American who had been a fighter pilot in the Gulf War (*Operation Desert Storm*). I don't think it would have been possible for me to find a better pilot . . . Pancho was the best.

The first meeting at dinner on Tuesday evening was relaxed and very enjoyable. The hotel restaurant was splendid, and the Mexican government officials were so warm and friendly I felt as if I had known them my whole life. As is the custom in Mexico, the business at hand was never even mentioned at that first meeting. There would be plenty of time for that. The more important thing was to get to know one another and to establish some sort of a relationship. In Mexico, relationships are paramount . . . they come before everything else. After a splendid dinner, I retired to my luxury suite and leisurely perused a piece of hotel literature that described the tour of San Cristobal we were scheduled to enjoy the following morning.

"Buenos Dias, Señor Lake, it's 9am. My name is Rosario, and I am the tour guide. I'm calling to let you know that the Secretaries are in the Hotel lobby, and we are just about to leave for the tour of San Cristobal. Would you like to join us?" Rosario was a gorgeous, 28-year-old Mayan woman with a Master's degree in history. "Yes, of course," I responded, "I'm on my way to the lobby right now. Thank you."

San Cristobal, a city of 150,000 people located in the highlands of the State of Chiapas, is nestled in a valley that is around 7,200 feet above sea level. The indigenous name for the city is *Jovel*; which means . . . *The Place in the Clouds*. The city is surrounded by mountain peaks and is about as picturesque a place as you'll ever see. In 2001, the Mexican Secretary of Tourism started a program that named certain places as being "Magical Villages" (*Pueblos Magicos)*. And, in 2010, the president of Mexico bestowed a great honor upon San Cristobal de Las Casas by giving it the title: "*El Mas Magico de Los Pueblos Magicos de Mexico*" (The Most Magical of the Magical Villages of Mexico).

The city appeared to be centered primarily on tourism along with the manufacturing and vending of artistic, native handicrafts. Because Rosario's tour vehicle was an open-air jeep, we had a particularly grand view of everything within our field of vision: "Una buena vista, verdad, Señor Lake!" shouted Rosario, "Si, Rosario . . . me gusta mucho!" ("A good view, right Mr. Lake!" "Yes, Rosario . . . I really like it!") Spanish, not Latin or Greek, was my true second language. Because of my parents' love for Spain and our much-used vacation home in Costa del Sol, I had been speaking Spanish for as long as I could remember.

Rosario took us to visit a couple of outdoor markets, as well as some very interesting museums. As we drove from place to place through the quaint, cobblestone streets of the old, Spanish colonial city, we passed scores of indigenous people. Never had I seen such a concentration of indigenous people in a given urban setting. No matter where you looked . . . there they were. Men, women, children, teenagers, the elderly . . . some dressed in western clothes, but most were wearing the traditional garb associated with their particular tribe.

While most were working as vendors, it was quite obvious that they were all pathetically poor and would never be able to sell enough of the various products they were peddling to lift them out of the impoverished condition they and their ancestors had known for centuries. No matter how hard they worked, life for them would continue to be a daily struggle for survival. And yet, they did not seem to be unhappy. I did not sense any bitterness or anger in them. To tell the truth, they seemed to be at peace . . . at least that's how they struck me.

I can't say that I was comfortable with them, however. In all honesty, I didn't really like them. They were much too different for me. They were so quiet, so mysterious . . . so poor! I suspected that their poverty was the aspect of their life most responsible for my negative feelings toward them. But as the morning wore on and there seemed to be no end to them, the truth began to settle in; I disliked the indigenous not simply because they were poor but because in the midst of their crushing poverty they radiated an authentic, interior peace that I, encrusted with layer upon layer of worldly riches . . . *did not have!*

The poverty of the indigenous, far from being "crushing" appeared to be liberating; whereas, my stupendous wealth had nothing of personal liberation in it. My many possessions were more like a ball and chain clamped tightly around my neck . . . or I should say, around my spirit! And although this "overdose" of contact with indigenous people caused me to have a new and valuable insight, I continued to reject them because I rationalized that they had no right to upset me and deprive me of the tiny shred of false peace that remained in the depths of my broken, worldly heart.

"I'd like to finish today's tour," announced Rosario, "by taking you to see the *Iglesia de Santo Domingo* (St. Dominic's Church), one of the most ornate churches in Latin America . . . and *La Catedral de San Cristobal Martir* (The Cathedral of St. Cristopher the Martyr); which was used by the famous Dominican Friar, Bartolome de Las Casas; the first bishop of Chiapas." I wasn't very interested in seeing churches at this time in my life. I had turned my back on God because I felt that he had turned his back on me. In fact, I hadn't been in a church since the plane crash. And although my life had been going downhill ever since, it never dawned on me that there might be a connection between those two occurrences.

The Secretaries, who were both Catholic, were very excited and happy that we were on our way to visit the churches, so I hid my reluctance and tried to act at least mildly enthusiastic: "OK . . . well . . . this will be my first time inside a Mexican church!" I was hoping this statement would serve as a disguise to cover up my faithless attitude. So far, things were going very well between me and the government representatives, and I didn't want to spoil it by coming across as the resident apostate. As far as they knew, I was a solid Catholic.

"Here we are, gentlemen," announced Rosario, "We have about 20 minutes to visit St. Dominic's . . . then we'll finish up with around 20 minutes at the Cathedral. I'll meet you right here in front of the Church in 20 minutes."

From an artistic point of view, the Church of St. Dominic was very impressive. The façade is a masterpiece of sculpture in the Baroque style. When you enter the Church you are greeted by an explosion of baroque art that unfolds in any direction you choose to gaze. I couldn't help but appreciate the enormous amount of work that must have gone into this vast display of very detailed and intricate art; not to mention the depth of faith and devotion it represented.

Nevertheless, I found it all quite disturbing. I felt that the people who built that church, unlike me, had *real* faith. The church made me feel "faithless." It raised my consciousness and caused me to become aware of how far I had wandered from the strong, innocent faith of my youth. There I was, sitting in a historic church considered to be a national treasure because of its plethora of religious art . . . and I was sad and confused. The Secretaries, on the other hand, were moving serenely about the church filled with enthusiasm, faith, and wonder.

I tried as best I could to work my way out of the church without being noticed. As I exited the church, I almost knocked over Rosario who was on her way in: "Oh! Excuse me! I'm sorry Rosario." I said. "That's OK Mr. Lake," replied Rosario, "Tell me; how did you like the church? You seem troubled?" Just what I didn't need at that moment; an intuitive woman looking directly into my eyes . . . or I should say . . . directly into my heart. But I instantly came up with what I thought was a darn good recovery: "You're very observant, Rosario. I was deeply moved by the sheer beauty of the church as well as the magnificent love of those who built it. So touched in fact that I felt I had to step outside to compose myself." "WOW, Mr. Lake! Que cosa hermosa! (What a beautiful thing!). Of the countless people I've brought to this church, never have I seen such a wonderful response! Obviously you have been gifted with an unusually profound and sincere faith. God must be very pleased with you!"

"Well, Rosario," I managed to say, although her phenomenally positive interpretation of what I had said left me practically speechless, "that's very kind of you. But I think it might be more accurate to see it this way; remember the saying: 'If you have faith the size of a mustard seed . . .' (Matthew 17:20), that's me, Rosario." "You are a blessed man, Mr. Lake . . . you have spiritual humility! The first Beatitude, Mr. Lake: 'Blessed are the poor in Spirit for theirs is the Kingdom of God!' I feel privileged to have had the opportunity of meeting you today, Mr. Lake."

As we walked back to the jeep, I realized that the despondent mood that had come over me so suddenly in the church was gone . . . completely gone! Somehow or other, the words Rosario spoke to me penetrated into the most hidden sectors of my heart, and restored it . . . instantly! "How did she do that?" I wondered to myself,

"Intuition doesn't cover it . . . there has to be more going on here." Something Rosario mentioned at the beginning of the tour was starting to sink in: "San Cristobal de Las Casas is . . . *El Mas Magico de Los Pueblos Magicos* (The Most Magical of the Magical Villages)."

"Last stop," Rosario shouted, "La Catedral de San Cristobal Martir!" As the Secretaries and I were crossing the Zócalo (also referred to as the *Plaza de La Paz*), en route to the main entrance of the Cathedral, I stopped to investigate a rather odd looking vendor's cart that was off to the side. Painted across the front of the relatively large cart were the words, "*Casa Bartolomé*". Staffing this makeshift, rolling store were a dozen indigenous young people ranging in age from around 10 to 16 years old. They were dressed in colorful, traditional outfits complete with straw hats. Hanging from every part of the cart, especially from the plywood canopy that shielded the cart from the blazing tropical sun, were handcrafted, wooden crucifixes. A number of the children, each carrying a few crucifixes, were missioned-out like traveling salesmen to various sections of the Zócalo.

The crucifixes came in many different sizes; the smallest being around 8 inches long, and the largest measured in at around 18 inches in length. They were all made of the same type of unfinished wood, but there was something very unique about these particular crucifixes. The crucified Christ was not a solid, separate material . . . he was painted directly on the wood.

And not only was the crucified Christ painted on the wooden crosses, the young vendors themselves were the artists who did the painting! What's more, as I began to chat with them I discovered that they were orphans and that *Casa Bartolomé* was an orphanage! I'm not sure why

I went over to their cart to begin with, but I think it may have been that, after my experience at St. Dominic's, I was hesitant to risk entering another church. I suspect, however, the more likely reason was that this rag-tag group of kids with their homemade store-on-wheels reminded me of *The Little Rascals* TV show I had grown up with. The only thing missing from this humorous scene was *Petey* . . . The Little Rascal's dog with the dark ring around his eye.

I had yet to purchase anything on the tour because, as I mentioned earlier, I was not very comfortable with the indigenous people and my tendency was to avoid unnecessary contact with them. But this group of orphans was different. For some reason, I was feeling a growing sense of solidarity with them . . . as if we had something in common. But how could that be possible? Then I realized what it was . . . I too was an orphan! Yes, there were huge differences; I was an adult and a multibillionaire. Nevertheless, I did know at the time what it felt like not to have parents. I shared this fact with them and the youngest one picked up a crucifix and said: "Si, Señor . . . no tener padres es una cruz que debemos llevar." ("Yes, Sir . . . not having parents is a cross we must carry). I immediately decided to purchase the 8-inch crucifix the little boy had shown me and passed a hundred dollar bill to the oldest of the group who was responsible for handling the cash box.

In perfect English, the boy responded: "Sir . . . the crucifix Rodrigo showed you sells for three dollars; I'm sorry but I can't change a hundred dollar bill." "That's OK," I replied, "give me three more crucifixes for my friends . . . and keep the change." The boy looked at me with a very confused expression on his face, as though he was saying to himself: "Although I'm very good at English, it is, after all, my third language. Perhaps I didn't understand this American correctly." I could sense his mental dilemma and so I said to him very clearly and very slowly: "I know it's a lot of money, but you may keep the change; consider it a donation." When my words finally sunk in, his face lit up with a smile that stretched from ear to ear: "Muchisimas Gracias, Señor! Padre Bill will be so happy . . . may God bless you and protect you!"

As I made my way in through the great doors of the Cathedral, toting my newly acquired cargo of crucifixes, hand-painted by Mayan orphans, I felt somewhat more worthy and much less intimidated by the prospect of being overcome with grief, guilt, and remorse. Perhaps, just to be safe, I should close my eyes; or look directly at the floor so as to eliminate altogether the possibility of another depressing "church" experience.

Since walking into an unknown church with my eyes closed was not a real option, and staring at the floor was a logistical impossibility, I entered the Cathedral like a normal human being and looked around. How happy I was to discover that the Cathedral was much less ornate than the previous church. The décor was not as "busy" and the entire feeling of the church was considerably calmer. "Just what the doctor ordered!" I thought, as I walked quietly down the center aisle realizing that I had been spared and so could now let down my guard and relax for the next 20 minutes.

I can't say that I did anything particularly interesting with my 20 minutes in one of the most historic churches in the world. All I did was sit peacefully in a pew. I didn't think of anything, and I didn't look at anything. I just sat there. Now for me, at that time in my life, sitting peacefully in a church and doing nothing at all was more historic than the Cathedral itself!

"Mr. Lake, I'm very sorry to disturb you," whispered Rosario, "I know that you have been caught up in an elevated state of prayer, but we are ready to return to the hotel now, and I didn't want to leave you behind, unless that's what you prefer. It's now 12 noon and your luncheon meeting begins at 1pm." "Elevated state of prayer?" I thought, "I don't think so!" But then again, who knows? I had no explanation for the tranquility I had been experiencing. I imagined I was just tired. Whatever it was that took place in that Cathedral was sufficiently pleasant that I decided right then and there to return the following day.

"Thanks, Rosario . . . I definitely want to go back to the hotel with the group." I replied. We exited the church, and I noticed that the "Little Rascals" were no longer working the Zócalo. When we arrived at the Jeep the Mexican officials were already there chatting away in Spanish. "Rosario . . . Gentlemen," I announced, "I have something here I would like to *share* with each of you." I took the crucifixes out of the bag and handed them out. "Gracias, Señor Lake!" exclaimed the officials, "How beautiful . . . Gracias!" Then Rosario said, "Mr. Lake, I don't know how to thank you. I will treasure this crucifix for the rest of my life! And the fact that it was crafted and painted by indigenous orphans makes it even more special!"

Dear reader . . . do you see what actually took place there? For the first time in memory, I freely shared something meaningful with others! And this sharing was from the heart; there was no hidden agenda . . . no strings attached! I didn't even reflect on it at the time; it all seemed so natural . . . so spontaneous. But something was indeed happening to me; my humanity was reemerging.

"What will you do with your new crucifix, Señor Lake?" asked Raul Ortega, the Secretary of the Environment. "A very wise person once told me," I responded, "that the best thing to do with a cross is to carry it. So I think I will take it with me wherever I go." Of course, I was referring to the little Mayan orphan who said: "Not having parents was a cross we must carry." "A very good idea, Mr. Lake . . . very good indeed!" replied Mr. Ortega.

CHAPTER FOUR

I was happy to be back in my hotel room so I could compose myself before the big meeting. As I lay there on the king size bed that had just been freshly made, my shoes off and my head propped up by 2 gigantic pillows . . . I began to wonder; what an unusual morning it had been. Who could have guessed that the notoriously self-absorbed Benjamin Lake would be donating money to indigenous people and buying crucifixes to give away as gifts? I reflected on the beautiful things Rosario said to me and how they touched my heart. I picked up my new crucifix and gazed into Jesus' eyes: "You're up to something, aren't you!" I said, "What are you doing with me?" I was tempted to tell him to leave me alone, but for some reason I couldn't get the words out. I was experiencing something altogether new, something I used to mock when I detected it in someone else. I was experiencing . . . meekness.

"That's impossible," I thought, "me . . . MEEK! Never! Not in a million years. It's against the Lake family rules. The indigenous, yes . . . they're meek; they've got it down to a science. But me . . . no way: it's not in my DNA." Then, suddenly, a new idea burst into my consciousness: "AHA!!! Yes! I know what it is . . . it's the altitude of this place; it's having an effect on me. Yes, of course, it's slowing me down . . . making me mellow: that's what's going on. Great! Now I know what's happening."

The luncheon meeting went well . . . at least as far as I was concerned. I'm not sure the Mexican government representatives would have assessed it quite that way, however. They were trying to persuade me to invest in their plan to develop ecotourism in the region. The Secretary of the Interior, Marcos Ruiz, was very articulate and convincing. As the saying goes, "He could have sold ice to an Eskimo!" But I went into the meeting with a closed mind. I knew what I wanted . . . and it wasn't ecotourism. Nevertheless, I played along leading them to think I was interested in what they had to say, but not yet thoroughly convinced.

"Gentlemen," I said, "I have listened to your presentation with great interest, but now, if you don't mind, I have a question." "Yes, of course, Mr. Lake," chimed in Señor Ruiz, "We would be happy to answer any questions you might have." I needed to probe a bit regarding the oil agenda, but I had to be careful not to reveal my bias. They were checking to see how open I was to their plan, now I wanted to see how open they might be to mine. The difference was that they could be forthright because their plan was very popular and "politically correct" . . . mine was neither.

"Based on your presentation, ecotourism is clearly a very fitting way to develop the economy in this region. But my question is this: is it the only way? Is there some other way that might be more lucrative? The numbers you quoted me are good . . . for Chiapas, MX. But by New York standards, they're not that impressive." I presented them with a "soft ball" question, hoping it wouldn't raise their antennae. Mr. Ruiz was only too happy to field this one: "Señor Lake . . . we have been studying this issue for many years now and, given the various factors involved, we have come to the conclusion that ecotourism is, without question, the single best way to develop this region. You have to keep in mind that the numbers we gave you cover only a 3-year projection. Ecotourism, over time, tends to expand and develop an economy exponentially."

That was all I needed to hear. With a response as clear and forceful as his, for me to push on further would have been a form of "negotiation suicide." "Sounds great, Mr. Secretary." I said, "Tell you what I'm going to do . . . I will take all of this info back to New York and my team and I will discuss it and review it very carefully. Give us a few weeks and I'll get back to you with an answer, OK? How does that sound?" I really should have gotten an academy award for that performance because I was not at all interested in their silly idea . . . and they didn't have a clue. Of course, their idea was excellent. My idea, on the other hand, was truly questionable. But, as Euripides, the great tragedian of classical Athens, wisely pointed out: *"Talk sense to a fool . . . and he calls you foolish!"*

"We enjoyed meeting you, Mr. Lake, and we look forward to hearing from you soon," declared Mr. Ruiz, speaking for his group. "Hopefully, we will be working with you in the not too distant future. Thank you for coming to Mexico to meet with us." "The pleasure was all mine, gentlemen. And as for coming to San Cristobal; I wouldn't have missed it for the world!" We shook hands, said "Adios," and thus ended what I considered to be one of the most useless business meetings I ever attended! The real, substantive meeting was to take place secretly later that evening. That clandestine, late-night dinner in *El*

Secreto, with the Secretary of Energy, Ricardo Villanueva, was the meeting I was literally "banking on."

I knew exactly where *Restaurante El Secreto* was because we passed it that morning while touring the *Centro Historico* (Historic Center) section of the city, and I made a mental note of its location with respect to the location of my hotel. It was only a few blocks away and easily within walking distance. As I relaxed in the hotel's beautiful, outdoor patio, enjoying the fresh, evening air and sipping a frosty glass of papaya juice, I began to wonder about the upcoming meeting. Given the steadfast position of the Secretary of the Interior regarding ecotourism, what could the Secretary of Energy possibly do to alter such a clear plan of action so as to open the way for petroleum development in the region? The answer to that question was the main reason I came to San Cristobal in the first place. I could only assume that there was some sort of an answer to the question, or the Secretary would not have requested the meeting. I was becoming very curious. There was a lot at stake . . . a lot hanging on the answer to that question.

It was 8:45pm and time to head over to *El Secreto.* What does one wear to a night time, clandestine meeting? I decided that what I had on would be just fine . . . a white cotton shirt, a camel colored sport coat, and jeans. Oh, and lest I forget . . . my new crucifix; which I was determined to take with me wherever I went. Not knowing exactly what to do with such a bulky item, I just slipped it between my belt and my pants a few inches to the right of the buckle. I didn't imagine something like that would go over well in Manhattan, but in San Cristobal de Las Casas, Mexico, I doubted if anyone would even notice. As I headed for the hotel lobby, an upsetting thought presented itself; I was quite sure the other government representatives had already left the city, but what if one of them had decided to remain behind at the hotel for another night and I bumped into him in the lobby or on the street? I prepared myself mentally for such a possibility but, as fate would have it, nothing of the sort came to pass.

As I made my way down the old, narrow, cobblestone streets that were illuminated with the soft glow of antique, gas street lights, I couldn't help but imagine, given the tumultuous political history of Mexico, that I was involved in a revolution and was on my way to a secret meeting with the leader of my faction. The walking and the night air worked wonders on my appetite, and I was looking forward to the outstanding Mexican food for which *El Secreto* was famous.

I found the street entrance to the restaurant and entered with a sense of mystery as my imagination continued to play with the idea of a revolution and a secret meeting. I strolled up to the maître d' and said exactly what Memphis told me to say, which, considering the playful state of mind I was in, seemed like a secret password: "Buenos Noches. My name is . . . Benjamin Lake." "Buenos Noches", said the maître d', "Bienvenidos (welcome), Señor Lake . . . please follow me." This was just fantastic . . . the "password" worked like a charm! I was really beginning to have fun with this whole affair. As Horace, an ancient Roman poet, wisely advised: *"Mix a little foolishness with your serious plans."*

My guide led me through the restaurant . . . which was just about at half capacity and, as I imagined, filled with spies of every sort . . . to a little section that was off to the side in the back of the main dining room. "Enjoy your dinner, Mr. Lake." said the maître d' as he ushered me into my chair. A man who looked to be around 45 years old and wearing khaki pants, a navy blue blazer, and a light blue oxford shirt, no tie and open at the collar, sprang to his feet: "Hello, Benjamin . . . I'm Ricardo; very good to meet you!" he said as we greeted one another. "Did you have any trouble finding the restaurant?" said Ricardo. "No . . . no trouble at all, Ricardo." I said, "And the walk here was great . . . I really enjoyed it." "I'm so glad to hear that, Benjamin!" replied Ricardo, "Well . . . let's sit and explore the menu. I think you are going to enjoy this restaurant . . . it's very special."

After a little "small talk" and some appetizers, we got down to the business at hand . . . the oil agenda. "How was your meeting this afternoon with Marcos Ruiz . . . did he show any openness to drilling?" questioned Ricardo. "No, absolutely none." I responded. "Yes, that's what I would expect, Benjamin. The government position is very clear on this point . . . no drilling in the Lacandon. You see Benjamin, the problem is not oil . . . the oil is there. And the problem is not really the government . . . the government would like to drill. The problem is the indigenous people and the environmentalists." Ricardo lowered his voice to a whisper as he spoke this last sentence because the waitress, who was a middle-aged indigenous woman, was approaching our table with our salads.

After the waitress moved away from our table, Ricardo continued: "You know, Benjamin . . . we have to be somewhat careful that our discussion is not overheard. This subject we are reviewing, as I believe you realize, is very sensitive. Having said this . . . it's extremely unlikely that our waitress knows English. In a tourist city like San

Cristobal, a person who knows English would generally have a much better position than working in a restaurant. So if we continue to speak in English we should be fine." "Yes, of course Ricardo," I said, "I agree . . . prudence in this matter is more than appropriate. English is fine with me." Having set the ground rules for the evening, Ricardo was now ready to present his basic thesis regarding the oil agenda.

"The biggest part of the problem, Benjamin, is not the environmentalists . . . it's the indigenous people; they are the real obstacle here. They're organized and vigorously opposed to drilling. To think that these primitive people, who are not even a product of western civilization, should have the capacity to stymie the progress of an entire nation is just not right." Ricardo lamented. "It's mind-boggling!" I said. "But what can be done? It seems that the decision in favor of ecotourism has already been made." "Yes," replied Ricardo, "the decision has been made. But it has not as of yet been implemented. The government needs investors. That's why they wanted to meet with you, Benjamin. But even if you were to decide against the investment, the government would still move forward with their plan."

"So then, Ricardo," I said, "is there a solution . . . is there some way around these obnoxious, stubborn people who thumb their collective noses at progress and development as though they deserved some sort of special treatment. Don't they realize that ever since Cortez landed in Veracruz, they have been a conquered people? We call the shots now, not them! As the saying goes: *to the victor go the spoils!*"

"Exactly, Benjamin!" replied Ricardo, all smiles, "I could not have said it any better! But we should keep in mind that, while they are very bold . . . a thoroughly obdurate people; this very trait . . . this obstinate boldness, could very well turn out to be their Achilles' heel."

"I'm not sure I understand you, Ricardo?" I replied cautiously. "Here's what I mean, Benjamin: right now the native people are reasonably popular . . . they have some support within Mexico . . . and even more in the United States and Europe. But public opinion would shift overnight if people were to see the indigenous as they really are . . . and not the glorified version that is so far from the truth. This is our only hope Benjamin; that in their boldness they will do something rash, and it will turn public opinion against them. When that happens, the government can forget about ecotourism because tourists will not want to have anything to do with the indigenous. And with public opinion against them, it will be much easier for the government to ignore them and to move forward with the only viable development option left . . . the oil agenda."

"Very good, Ricardo . . . I think I see where you're going with this; we watch and wait, patiently. As Thucydides, a Greek general and historian said: *Ignorance is bold . . . and knowledge reserved.* How likely do you think it is, Ricardo, that they will do something sufficiently rash to alter the playing field, as it were?"

"Well, as it is, Benjamin . . . I would think it to be very likely; considering how their political movement is growing in leaps and bounds and they are becoming more animated and outspoken with each passing day. I would imagine that within the next year or so they will cross the line in some way or another." "Let's hope so, Ricardo," I added, "Developing this untapped oil reserve is an opportunity of a lifetime, and that's the very thing

Praetergressus Bank specializes in; let's not miss it! We have to be prepared so that when the opportunity presents itself we are one step ahead of the competition and ready to strike while the iron is hot."

"I couldn't agree more, Benjamin! As for me . . . I'm more than ready . . . I'm biting at the bit! How about you Benjamin . . . are you ready?" "For an opportunity like this, Ricardo . . . as the saying goes: I was born ready!" "Fantastic!" exclaimed Ricardo, "Then I think we can say, Benjamin, that this was a very productive and truly successful meeting; in honor of which I would ask you to let me have the privilege of paying the restaurant bill." "Not on your life, Ricardo . . . no way!" I declared, "It was my pleasure and my treat." "Thank you, Benjamin, you are very kind. I will be returning to Mexico City first thing in the morning. You mentioned, Benjamin, that you would be leaving on Friday . . . will you be touring again tomorrow?" questioned Ricardo. "No . . . tomorrow is a free day," I responded, "but I'm planning to walk down to the Cathedral on my own for a little visit. Other than that, I'll just play it by ear." "Excellent!" exclaimed Ricardo.

CHAPTER FIVE

The following morning, after a hearty Mexican breakfast of scrambled eggs, chorizo, refried beans and flour tortillas, I was on my way to the Cathedral for another session, I hoped, of "elevated prayer" . . . or whatever it was that put me into something resembling a semi-comatose state. As I approached the Zócalo in front of the Cathedral, I could see that the orphans had already arrived and were spread out strategically as they had been the day before.

"Señor, Señor!" called out one of the orphans as he ran up to greet me, "Do you remember me? I'm the one who sold you the crucifix yesterday. My name is Antonio. Padre Bill, the Franciscan priest in charge of the orphanage, told me to tell you that he is very grateful for your generous donation and that he offered the holy mass for you this morning! He also told me to tell you that whenever you come to San Cristobal you will have a home here . . . the orphanage is your home!"

"Yes . . . I remember you, Antonio," I replied, "and please tell Fr. Bill I appreciate the mass and his gracious hospitality." "I will tell him, Señor," said Antonio. "But before you go into the Cathedral to pray, could I ask you, what is your name?" "My name is Benjamin." I replied.

"Thank you, Señor Benjamin . . . now that we know your name, we can pray for you. Padre Bill says that we orphans have to stick together and help one another!"

"Upon entering the Cathedral, I immediately began to sense that deep, penetrating peace that had tranquilized me the day before. But this time I felt as though this inexplicable tranquility was leading me somewhere. I walked very slowly down the center aisle, and I began to feel light on my feet, almost as if I were floating a fraction of an inch above the floor. The Cathedral was poorly lit and filled with the delightful fragrance of fresh flowers and exotic incense. There were candles flickering here and there, and scattered about in various pews were about 5 or 6 elderly, indigenous women praying. Some were quietly praying the rosary while others seemed to be in the same state of "elevated prayer" I had experienced the day before.

I passed a number of pews that appeared to be perfect for me to sit in, but for some strange reason I did not enter any of them; I just continued to move forward not really knowing where I was going or what I was looking for. As I "drifted" through this dark, cavernous cathedral, beclouded with smoke from a galaxy of burning candles, I suddenly found myself face to face with a massive, wooden door. It appeared to be a side door leading to the outside. How strange . . . I had come to visit the Cathedral, but now, not knowing why, I was on my way out of the Cathedral.

I pushed the door and it opened unto the side courtyard of the Cathedral. I felt as though I was being called forth from the mysterious shadows of the Cathedral into the radiant light of day and for a split second, the image of Lazarus emerging from the tomb ran through my mind. I looked to my left and saw a sign which read . . . *Templo de San Nicolás*. I knew immediately . . . intuitively . . . that whatever or whoever it was that was guiding me wanted me to go into that little church attached to the back of the Cathedral.

Upon entering San Nicolás, a pleasant feeling of relaxation descended upon me, as though I had finally arrived at the destination to which I was being led. Compared to the Cathedral, the interior of the church was refreshingly simple. So much so that I loved it immediately! Clearly, this was a low-budget addition to the Cathedral that must have served some purpose in its day. All I really knew was that this simple little church was definitely "my speed;" this was the kind of church that could speak to my battered heart.

Everything about the church was pretty much "bare bones"; or to put it another way . . . "No Frills!" I could see right away that, not surprisingly, I was the only person in the church. Given the number of extraordinary churches in San Cristobal, what tourist would use any of their precious, limited time to visit a humble church like San Nicolás? I would not have visited it, either, had I not been drawn to it by some kindly force unbeknownst to me.

As I moved forward from the back of the church toward the sanctuary in the front, I decided to turn into a pew and take a seat. The pews were so ordinary that it appeared as though they could have been constructed in someone's backyard. This being the case, why was this simple chapel so attractive to me? Why was I there? Who or what was it that led me there? I settled into my seat, and as I continued to relax I began to hear more distinctly the remarkably beautiful birdsong that was taking place outside the church. It had been a long time since I had been sufficiently recollected to take note of something as simple as the sound of birds singing.

Listening to such delightful music, the source of which I could not see, touched my heart in such a way that I felt I had to kneel . . . and so, I did. And as I knelt there, gazing in the direction of the sanctuary and the humble retablo behind it, I had this feeling that I was not alone . . . that someone was present there with me; not in the flesh . . . but spiritually. It was fleeting . . . but it registered on my soul. Struck by the beauty of that precious moment, I closed my eyes and lowered my head in silent prayer and thanksgiving.

When I opened my eyes, I was looking down at the seat of the pew in front of me and was surprised to see a rather old, antique-looking book sitting there. My first thought was that it probably belonged to someone and therefore the proper thing to do would be to leave it alone and not touch it. Perhaps it was personal . . . someone's diary or something. I looked up and down that pew, as well as my own pew, and there was not a single book anywhere. Sensing that somehow this book was put there for me, without giving it any further thought I simply reached down, picked it up, opened it and began to read.

"LATIN! I can't believe it!" I was saying to myself. "This book is written in classical Latin! Without question, this book was meant for me!" I cracked open the book and looked intently at the page before me. The first sentence my eyes fell upon was this: *Fecisti nos ad te, Domine, et inquietum est cor nostrum donec requiescat in te* (You have made us for yourself, Lord, and our hearts are restless until they rest in you).

I sat back in the pew in a state of wonder and pondered the profound meaning of the Latin words I had just read from a book that came out of nowhere . . . in a church I wasn't even looking for! I sat there for a good 15 minutes allowing the message of those words to sink deeply into my heart. Finally, it occurred to me that I didn't even know the title or the author of the mysterious book that just spoke to my heart in such a powerful way.

The cover was very old and worn, so I held the book at different angles until I could just barely make out the title; *CONFESSIONES,* was the Latin title on the cover. "Could this actually be St. Augustine's *Confessions?*" I thought to myself. I turned to the opening pages and right away, my original guess was confirmed; amazingly . . . I was holding in my hands a rare copy of St. Augustine's *Confessions* in the original Latin.

My Classical Studies Program at Harvard pretty much ignored St. Augustine. He was considered to be relatively boring and unimportant . . . compared to the likes of Virgil, Ovid, Horace, Cicero, Terence, Seneca, and Marcus Aurelius. Therefore, I never paid much attention to him. Of course, I knew he wrote in Latin . . . but I didn't know his Latin was as refined and as beautiful as that which I was reading. I knew he had written a book called *Confessions* . . . but, in truth, I had no idea what it was about. I imagined it to be some dull treatise concerning the Sacrament of Reconciliation.

I really don't know how long I was sitting there, but at some point I decided to head back to the hotel. I picked up my newly discovered treasure, St. Augustine's *Confessions,* and slowly walked out of a little chapel I would not soon forget. As I was pushing the door open to exit the church, I looked back inside, half expecting (based on the joy that was now radiating within me) to see winged angels fluttering about. But the chapel was as calm and peaceful as it had been when I first entered.

As I walked along the side plaza of the great Cathedral on my way back to the main Zócalo, I felt a new spring in my step. The air seemed more fragrant, the sunlight more pleasing, and the sound of the birds and the children more delightful. I waved to the children from *Casa Bartolomé* as I passed them and their home-made, mobile store . . . a scene which was right out of an episode from *Spanky and Our Gang,* and proceeded across the busy Zócalo.

When I reached the street called *16 de Septiembre,* which is the street that leads back to the hotel, I noticed a black, Mercedes sedan moving very slowly, close to the curb, as if it were about to park. I hesitated for a moment to observe it, and it came to a stop directly in front of me. Suddenly, I sensed 2 men approaching me rather quickly, one to my left and one from behind me. I didn't think anything of it, imagining they were in a hurry to get somewhere, so I just stood still allowing them to pass. But they didn't pass; they closed in and came right up to me.

The one who approached from my left stood directly in front of me, while the other one positioned himself around 3 feet behind me with his arms folded across his chest . . . as though it was his job to keep me from escaping should I attempt to do so. Both men were rough looking individuals dressed in black cowboy boots, blue jeans, black T-Shirts, black sport coats and dark sunglasses. I immediately had the feeling that these men, along with the Mercedes, were trouble, and I was definitely in some kind of real danger.

"Señor Lake . . . we are the Mexican Federal Police. Your life is in danger and you must come with us. Please get in the car." said the man in front of me, as he opened the back door of the car. "Oh . . . you're *Federales?*" I questioned, "I'd like to see some I.D." Get in the car NOW!

This is an emergency . . . I will show you I.D. when we are in the car." was the stranger's excited retort. "I'm not going anywhere until I see some I.D." I declared.

At that moment, the man drew back the right side of his sport coat to reveal a sidearm: "Get in the car!" he said. With those words, the man behind me put his hands on my shoulders. The instant I felt those bulky hands on my shoulders I spun to the left and took off for the Cathedral like an Olympic Gold Medalist. The thug who was supposed to thwart my escape lunged out at me and managed to get his right hand on my waist but all he came away with was my new, wooden crucifix . . . which had been tucked between my belt and my pants. He glanced at it for an instant and, amidst a torrent of expletives, threw it violently to the ground. "Saved by *my* sidearm . . . the crucifix!" was all I could think of as I raced toward the Cathedral.

"Get him! Go, Go . . . Get him! Don't let him get away! RAPIDO!" cried the mysterious man behind the wheel of the Mercedes. The Zócalo was packed with tourists and vendors who created a field of endless obstacles that was certainly working in my favor as I continued to put distance between myself and my pursuers. I'm not sure why I headed for the Cathedral but I suppose it was an instinctive sense that I would find safety and protection there.

While I was pumped up with adrenalin and running for my life something else was going on in the Zócalo. Without my being aware of it, the children from *Casa Bartolomé* had witnessed the whole incident and went into action immediately: "Rodrigo, go retrieve Benjamin's crucifix." ordered Antonio . . . as he assumed the position of acting leader of the orphans. "Carlitos . . . go and get the license plate number of that black Mercedes. Be careful . . . don't let anyone see you!"

"The rest of you, come with me. We have to rescue Benjamin, a brother orphan, from these men . . . whoever they are." Antonio was 16 years old and as good a commander of an "orphan rescue operation" as you could ever hope to find: "Miguelito," said Antonio, "I want you and the boys to push the cart up there, to the side door of the Cathedral. I'm going to run ahead and enter the Cathedral. If I find Benjamin, I will lead him back out the side door where you will be waiting. Then we will hide him in the cart and take him back with us to the orphanage where he will be safe." "OK, Antonio," responded Miguelito, "We will be in position and waiting for you and Benjamin. Vaya con Dios!"

CHAPTER SIX

Antonio entered the cathedral slowly and as quietly as possible, barely even opening the door. It was midday and the Cathedral was already filled with tourists. He took one small step forward and then allowed his gaze to survey the full span of the Cathedral interior. He spotted the two thugs near the main entrance doing essentially the same thing he was doing. But he did not see Benjamin. He was about to give up when he moved back against the wall so that a tour group could pass. There, in with the group, was Benjamin! He was using the group as cover and was looking back in the direction of the main entrance so he could keep track of his pursuers.

"Pssst! Pssst! Benjamin . . . over here!" whispered Antonio. "Antonio! I'm sorry but I can't talk with you now . . . I have to hide. I'm being chased by 2 kidnappers!" I said in a low, terrified voice, as I crouched down against the wall. "I know," responded Antonio, "that's why I'm here . . . we're going to rescue you! We're like your Marines . . . we never leave a fellow orphan behind! Follow me out the door. The boys are waiting outside with the cart. We will hide you in the cart and take you back to the orphanage with us." Antonio looked around to make sure the kidnappers were not watching . . . then he put his index finger up to his lips: "Shishhh! Stay with me . . . here we go."

Antonio opened the door no more than 12 inches and we squeezed through to make our escape. Right there on the pavement in front of us were the boys and the "getaway car." Two of the boys were already in position, holding open the heavy, canvas curtains that covered the main storage area of the cart. I crawled inside and they immediately closed and secured the curtains. "YA! Vamanos!" (NOW! Let's go!), directed Antonio. I didn't even have a chance to discover a comfortable position yet and off we went; rolling down the back streets of San Cristobal on our way to *Casa Bartolomé.*

"Benjamin . . . are you OK in there?" inquired Antonio. "Yeah . . . I'm fine, Antonio." I responded, "This isn't exactly a luxury vehicle! But it sure beats that black Mercedes!" "Just hang on, Benjamin," said Antonio, "it won't be long now . . . maybe another 15 minutes or so. I instructed the boys not to speak to anyone along the way because we're not going to stop moving until we reach the orphanage."

When we were about a block away from the *Casa*, the little ten year old, Rodrigo, made a funny comment: "Hey, Mr. Benjamin?" "Yes Rodrigo . . . what is it?" I said. "Mr. Benjamin, you escaped the kidnappers; but now you are in the hands of the orphans. Does that make *us* kidnappers?" "No, Rodrigo . . . you're not kidnappers." "But," questioned Rodrigo, "if we're not kidnappers . . . then what are we?" "You're angels, Rodrigo! Yep . . . that's what you are . . . angels!"

Casa Bartolomé was on 2 acres of land at the terminus of a dead end street and was circumscribed by a white, 8-foot, cement block wall. The physical plant consisted of 3 structures that were connected by 2 cloister-like breezeways. The 3 buildings were lined up in a row, dead center in the property. The building in the middle contained all the common rooms, such as the main chapel, dining room, kitchen, offices, living room, class rooms, and recreation room.

The building on the right was the orphan's dormitory, and the building on the left was a Franciscan Friary. The orphans rolled the cart up the cement driveway to the main entrance directly in front of the middle building and stopped just short of the big, solid metal gate: "We are here, Benjamin," whispered Antonio, "but don't come out yet. Wait until we open the gate and get inside. Then wait until we close the gate. After we close the gate, it will be safe for you to come out." "OK, Antonio," I said, "but let me know as soon as you close the gate because if I stay in here any longer I'll be in a chiropractor's office twice a week for the rest of my life!"

"You can come out now, Benjamin." called out Antonio. I pushed aside the canvas curtains and almost went into cardiac arrest! Right in front of me, about six inches from my face, was the enormous, white snout of a 150-pound, Pyrenean Mountain Dog (*Great Pyrenees*)! He proceeded to lick my face as the boys howled with laughter: "Hold on to him, Benjamin" said Rodrigo, "he's very smart . . . he'll help you get out of there; that's one of his jobs!" I grabbed hold of his harness and sure enough, he pulled me out and the boys helped me to my feet.

"Good boy, Montecito (little mountain)!" said Antonio, "Now that you have met Montecito, our Chief of Security, it's time to meet Padre Bill . . . the Director of *Casa Bartolomé.*" Antonio told the boys that he would introduce me to Fr. Bill, and they were to go about their normal schedule: "Boys . . . don't say a word to anyone about Benjamin." instructed Antonio, "If the kidnappers find out he is here . . . we will all be in danger." "Benjamin? Who's that?" said Miguelito. "Perfect, Miguelito!" replied Antonio, "You see boys . . . nothing unusual happened today. It was a perfectly normal day."

Antonio led me into the friary and told me to wait there in the parlor while he went to find Fr. Bill. "Well . . . hello there! So you're Benjamin!" said Fr. Bill as he entered the room. "Benjamin Lake, Father . . . good to meet you!" Fr. Bill was in his early seventies, around 5'8", chubby and bald as an egg, with a very cheerful, pleasant countenance. He was buried under a traditional, brown, Franciscan habit with a long, white rope tied around the waist. It would be hard to imagine a friendlier personality. I felt as though he was an old friend and was very much at ease in his presence.

"Thank you for everything you did today, Antonio," said Fr. Bill, "I'm very proud of you! Why don't you join the other children now while Benjamin and I have a little chat. I'll meet with you and the boys in a little while." "Si, Padre . . . hasta la vista!" (Yes, Father . . . see you later!), replied Antonio as he turned for the door. "Oh, Antonio?" said Benjamin, "Thank you. You saved my life today!" "God watches over the orphans, Señor Benjamin," replied Antonio, "It says that in the Bible!"

"Benjamin," began Fr. Bill, "Antonio told me about the attempted kidnapping today. Other than the fact that you gave us a very generous donation yesterday, I really don't know anything about you. Why would someone try to kidnap you?" "Well, Fr. Bill," replied Benjamin, "it might have something to do with the fact that I own the largest, private bank in the USA." "Oh! Yes . . . of course!" said Fr.

Bill, "You're *that* Benjamin Lake. I'm so sorry about your parents . . . I read about the tragic plane crash. Now I understand why Antonio has been referring to you as a brother orphan."

As Fr. Bill was speaking, a woman came in the front door and I recognized her as the waitress at the restaurant the night before. "Good afternoon, Esperanza," said Fr. Bill, as we both rose to our feet, "Mr. Lake . . . this is Esperanza Santos. Esperanza is an ESL (*English as a Second Language*) teacher and has volunteered to teach our children English." With those words, I thought I would stop breathing. Judging by her body language and facial expression, it was clear that she had overheard and understood much of what Ricardo and I had been discussing in *El Secreto*. I extended my hand . . . but she refused to extend hers. In fact, she took a step back . . . as though I was contaminated with some sort of deadly disease and she didn't want to get too close.

"Fr. Bill," said Esperanza, in an excited, angry tone, "do you know who this man is? He is an enemy of my people! He was at the restaurant last night with another man named Ricardo and they were plotting and scheming about how they could undermine the stubborn, primitive, ignorant, bold, obnoxious, did I leave anything out, Mr. Lake . . . oh yes . . . CONQUERED indigenous people, so that the Americans would then be able to drill for oil in the *Montes Azules Reserve*! What is he doing here in your house? I hope he came here to go to confession!"

"Actually, Esperanza," replied Fr. Bill, "he is here because someone tried to kidnap him today, right in front of the Cathedral . . . and the orphans rescued him and brought him home with them." "Give him back to the kidnappers!" yelled Esperanza, "He deserves to be kidnapped! It was probably God's will that he be kidnapped . . . the boys should not have interfered!"

"Benjamin," asked Fr. Bill, "is what Esperanza just said . . . about the restaurant and the meeting . . . is it true?" "Yes, Fr. Bill . . . every word of it, I'm ashamed to say." "He is *not* ashamed, Fr. Bill!" cried out Esperanza, "Don't believe him! He is a typical, wealthy, American businessman . . . filled with reckless, insatiable greed! In Spanish, we have a name for someone like him; he is . . . *sin vergüenza* (without shame)! And to think my daughter had such a high opinion of him! He is not only greedy, he is a fraud and a deceiver! And he doesn't care who he hurts, so long as he can make money!

Having practically exhausted herself with such an intense emotional outburst, Esperanza quickly made her exit out the front door, leaving a mortified billionaire and an utterly perplexed friar standing there in the center of the parlor staring at each other: "Fr. Bill," I asked, "who is Esperanza's daughter?" "Esperanza's daughter is a beautiful young lady named Rosario. She works as a tour guide and is a history tutor for our orphans. Perhaps you met her at the hotel?" "Yes!" I blurted out, as though yet another "bomb" had just been dropped on me, "I believe I did meet her at my hotel . . . the Hotel Bo; she was our tour guide on Wednesday." Yes, Benjamin," said Fr. Bill, "That was her." "She seems like a very special person." I said. "Oh . . . indeed she is!" responded Fr. Bill with conviction, "She and her mother are Lay Dominicans. They are true missionary disciples, Benjamin . . . believe me! Because of the history of San Cristobal, you will find many Dominicans here. Rosario will be in the main building this evening at 6:30pm to give the children a history lesson. And if I'm not mistaken, tonight she will be speaking about the holy Dominican Bishop . . . Bartolomé de Las Casas."

"Benjamin," said Fr. Bill, "there is much for us to discuss. But first . . . I think you should take a siesta; you look exhausted . . . you've had quite a traumatic day!" "You're right, Father . . . I'm so wiped-out I can barely think straight. I need to rest. And as the Roman poet, Virgil, said: *Better times perhaps await us who are now wretched.*" "Ah . . . Virgil! Author of the *Aeneid;* do you know Latin, Benjamin?" questioned Fr. Bill. "Yes, Father. I have a PhD in Classical Studies from Harvard." "Wonderful, Benjamin! That's fantastic!" exclaimed Fr. Bill, "Now remember, Benjamin . . . you are most welcome here; this is your home in San Cristobal. Why don't we meet back here at 4:30pm and continue our discussion. Come with me and I'll show you your room."

CHAPTER SEVEN

"Buenos tardes, Benjamin (good afternoon, Benjamin)!" said Fr. Bill, "How was your siesta?" "I wish I could say it was great," I answered, "but it wasn't. I'm still upset because of that nightmarish encounter I had with the kidnappers today." "Yes, of course you are! Would you like to talk about it?" offered Fr. Bill. "There's so much I'd like to discuss with you," I said, "I guess the attempted kidnapping is as good a place as any to jump in. The thing that bothers me most about the kidnapping attempt is that it is partly my fault. After the loss of my parents, I turned to the world for consolation. I threw myself into a thoroughly degenerate lifestyle, hoping to drown my spiritual pain with worldly pleasure. And since my life had become so debauched and dissolute, I dismissed my security people because I was too embarrassed to have body guards around to witness my moral decline. If my security had been with me today, those kidnappers would have never gotten near me."

"You're probably right, Benjamin," said Fr. Bill, "But if you think about it . . . today you had the best security you could possibly have; God himself was watching over you! Here you are, sitting in front of me, a little shaken up . . . but not a hair on your head was hurt. I offered mass for you this morning . . . and the boys have been praying for you since they met you yesterday. The Lord goes before us, Benjamin. He was with you today. Now tell me, Benjamin, I'm just curious; what were you doing at the Cathedral this morning?"

"I'm so glad you asked me that, Fr. Bill," I said, "because this is what I really need to talk to you about. Yesterday, before the attempted kidnapping, I had a very mysterious spiritual experience." "Good, Benjamin," said Fr. Bill, "I'm listening . . . tell me all about it." I continued: "I went into the Cathedral for a little visit and felt as if I was being led somewhere. My intention was to sit in one of the pews, but instead, I found myself outside and on my way to a little church attached to the back of the cathedral." "San Nicolas?" interjected Fr. Bill. "Yes . . . precisely. I walked into the chapel and immediately felt a sense of peace and relaxation . . . as though I had arrived at the place to which I was being led."

"And then?" inquired Fr. Bill. "I chose a pew and sat down. I was sitting there very peacefully when I began to hear the most glorious birdsong I have ever heard. It touched my heart so deeply that I was moved to assume a kneeling position. I knelt there for a while and just gazed at the sanctuary. Suddenly I had this feeling that I was not alone . . . that someone was there with me . . . spiritually. I closed my eyes and lowered my head in humble thanksgiving. When I opened my eyes, I saw on the bench in front of me this very book that I'm holding up for you to see now. I picked it up and discovered that it was St. Augustine's *Confessions* . . . in Latin! Now Father . . . what are the chances that all of these things just 'happened'?"

"None, Benjamin! What took place next?" asked Fr. Bill. "When I opened the book, the first sentence I read was this: *You have made us for yourself, Lord, and our hearts are restless until they rest in you.* I sat there and meditated on those words, which sank so deeply into my heart, mind, and soul that I can't even begin to tell you, Fr. Bill. Then I left the chapel, walked across the Zócalo and ran into the kidnappers."

"What a blessing, Benjamin . . . pure grace! Not the kidnappers! I'm referring to the discovery of the book." exclaimed Fr. Bill, "Benjamin, tell me . . . have you ever read Augustine's *Confessions*?" "No, Fr. Bill." answered Benjamin. "Do you know anything about St. Augustine . . . I mean, anything about his life?" asked Fr. Bill. "No," replied Benjamin.

"Benjamin . . . you and Augustine have much in common. When Augustine was a young man, he made some bad choices and fell into a worldly, hedonistic lifestyle similar to the wild life you chose to live when you lost your parents. One day when he was relaxing in a garden, he heard children singing and was moved to open a Bible that just happened to be nearby. The first sentence he saw convinced him that he must change his ways. The book you found in the chapel is an autobiographical account of the entire story of St. Augustine's life and conversion!" "Do you know, Father," I added, "at first, I wasn't going to touch the book because I thought it might be someone's personal diary. Based on what you just said, my initial intuition was actually correct!"

"Yes, Benjamin!" replied Fr. Bill, "but something . . . or someone . . . moved you to pick it up. Benjamin . . . I think it was *someone*; I think it was St. Augustine himself! Just look at the similarities: he was in a garden . . . you were in a chapel; he heard children singing . . . you heard birds singing; he picked up the Bible . . . you picked up his

Confessions; he opened the book and his eyes fell upon a sentence that touched his heart very deeply; you opened the book and your eyes fell upon a sentence that touched your heart very deeply. And something else Benjamin that you are probably not aware of yet; after Augustine had this beautiful, transformative experience, the Spirit led him to a Catholic clergyman . . . St. Ambrose. I think the same Spirit led you here today so you could share this marvelous story with me."

"Fr. Bill, this is really amazing stuff!" I exclaimed, "And you actually expect me to sleep tonight? After hearing what you just shared, I don't think I'll ever sleep again!"

"It's all very mysterious, Benjamin," said Fr. Bill, "but it seems to me that St. Augustine is watching over you and has reached out to you today. By the way Benjamin, the chapel where all this happened today . . ." "San Nicolas?" I interjected. "Yes," replied Fr. Bill, "Do you know who built it?" "No," I answered. *"Augustinian* monks!" replied Fr. Bill with a big smile! "And do you know why it was built, Benjamin?" "No, Fr. Bill." I answered. "It was built to be used specifically by the indigenous . . . that's why it's so beautifully simple!" related Fr. Bill.

"Now Benjamin, there are some practical matters that we really need to get to. We can come back to this spiritual discussion later on this evening. I know some of these things can be difficult to face, but I think you will agree; you can't go back to the hotel because the kidnappers will probably be waiting for you there. So, until we know more about the identity of these criminals, it would be best for you to remain here at the orphanage. And it wouldn't be advisable to contact the police just yet because often enough, here in Mexico, the police are involved in the kidnappings. Considering the fact that you were attacked in broad daylight in front of the cathedral, at a time when the Zócalo is filled with tourists . . . I strongly suspect police, and possibly government involvement; which is why I would also suggest not making any phone calls back to the states . . . they might be intercepted. There's also the remote possibility that someone in your home office is on the kidnapper's payroll."

"But if that's the case, Fr. Bill," I said, "wouldn't my presence here put you and the orphans in danger?" "Yes." answered Fr. Bill, "But there is a solution; it's called . . . a disguise; or better yet, a new identity! You are going to be Brother Matthew for the next few weeks. Here is your Franciscan habit . . . go ahead, put it on . . . wear it at all times. Also . . . you will need to shave your head and grow a full beard. I met with the boys earlier and explained to them that you are now a Franciscan and your name is Br. Matthew. Luckily, this is a relatively small orphanage, Benjamin. We only have 12 boys ranging in age from 10 to 16 . . . all of them are Lacandon Maya. So, it shouldn't be that difficult to keep your real identity secret. I have called Esperanza and asked her not to mention your presence here to anyone. She said she already realized that if the kidnappers found out that you were here it would put all of us in danger. Also . . . she advised her daughter, Rosario, regarding this matter. So, you can relax . . . Br. Matthew: God is watching over you . . . he has a plan for you!"

"Wow!" I said to myself, "and I thought New York City was fast-paced? San Cristobal is completely off the chart! In the course of around 6 hours, I've gone from being a disgraceful, materialistic billionaire . . . to being a poor, Franciscan friar named Br. Matthew!" We were just about to finish up our conversation when we heard a gentle knock on the door: "Come in Rodrigo!" yelled Fr. Bill. "I know his knock." whispered Fr. Bill. In walked Rodrigo with Antonio right behind him: "Br. Matthew," Antonio began, "after the kidnapper threw away your crucifix today, Rodrigo ran over and recovered it. When we heard that you would be wearing the Franciscan habit, Rodrigo suggested that we fix the crucifix up for you as a gift. Rodrigo . . . you can present Br. Matthew with his crucifix now."

Rodrigo walked up to me and handed me my crucifix, which he had been holding behind his back. The children had made a small hole in the top of the crucifix so that a thin, leather strap could be attached, enabling the crucifix to be worn around the neck. "Thank you, Rodrigo!" I said, and immediately proceeded to put the crucifix on so he and Antonio could see how it looked. "What do you think guys?" I said. "It's beautiful!" they exclaimed.

"What a marvelous surprise, boys!" said Fr. Bill, "Well, it's just about time for Rosario's presentation on Bartolomé de Las Casas. Are you familiar with his life, Br. Matthew?" inquired Fr. Bill. "No, Fr. Bill. I've heard the name . . . but I know nothing about the man." If you feel up to it," said Fr. Bill, "I think you might enjoy hearing about his life." "Do I have time to shave my head first?" I asked. "Yes, Br. Matthew . . . you have at least 15 minutes." replied Fr. Bill.

I sat quietly in the back of the classroom and listened to Rosario as she taught the children about the holy Dominican Bishop after whom their city was named (San Cristobal *de Las Casas*). I was absolutely spellbound by what I was hearing about this amazing man! He started out as a colonist and, like all the other colonists, ran "roughshod" over the indigenous so that his plantations would produce huge profits. But the Lord opened his eyes and touched his heart and he became the first officially appointed *"Protector of the Indians."* But that wasn't enough for him . . . he wanted to do more for the poor. So he gave away his worldly possessions, became a Dominican friar, and spent the rest of his life working tirelessly to improve the lives of the indigenous people as best he could. The process for his beatification was begun in 2002.

Amazingly, I did not detect in Rosario any animosity toward me, and I was very surprised to see that she was wearing the crucifix I gave her. If I sensed anything in her, it was pity. Perhaps sitting in the back of the children's classroom in a Franciscan habit with my head roughly shaved made me look like I was doing penance . . . in "sackcloth and ashes"! When Rosario was finished with her presentation she dismissed the students and walked over to talk with me: "Good evening, Brother Matthew . . . did you enjoy the presentation?" "Oh, Yes!" I responded, "You did a fantastic job!" "What are your thoughts regarding de Las Casas?" she asked. "He was a wonderful man, Rosario." I replied, "I was deeply moved by his beautiful life."

"I'm very glad to hear that, Brother Matthew." said Rosario. "Brother . . . did you see the news this evening?" "No, Rosario, I didn't." "Come with me, Brother," directed Rosario in a somewhat excited tone, "We have to talk with Fr. Bill right away!"

Rosario knocked on Fr. Bill's door: "Fr. Bill its Rosario, I have to talk with you. It's important!" "OK, Rosario . . . I'll meet you in the parlor." answered Fr. Bill. When Fr. Bill entered the parlor, Rosario greeted him and said: "Fr. Bill . . . did you see the evening news?" "No, Rosario," responded Fr. Bill, "I didn't have a chance. What's going on?"

"The police chief of San Cristobal had a press conference and said a ransom note was found in Benjamin Lake's hotel room stating that Mr. Lake had been abducted by the indigenous people and was being held for a ransom of one hundred million US dollars!"

"Benjamin . . . I mean, Br. Matthew," inquired Fr. Bill, "the men who tried to kidnap you . . . did they appear to be indigenous?" "No," I replied. "Rosario . . . can you think of any indigenous group that would attempt a kidnapping for ransom like this?" inquired Fr. Bill. "No, Fr. Bill . . . none that I know of." "But if it wasn't an indigenous group . . . who was it?" I asked. "Good question!" answered Fr. Bill, "And whoever was behind it . . . why would they want the indigenous to be blamed?"

"Perhaps the real kidnappers wanted to send the authorities on a wild goose chase?" I suggested. "Yes, Br. Matthew . . . that's probably exactly what's going on here." observed Fr. Bill. "What do you think, Rosario?" asked Fr. Bill. "I agree, Fr. Bill,' responded Rosario, "but doesn't it strike both of you as odd that the ransom note was placed in the hotel room *before* they had successfully captured the individual they targeted?" "Yes . . . very strange indeed!" I said, "It makes them seem like clumsy amateurs." "Unless," observed Fr. Bill, "as Polonius said to Hamlet: *Though this be madness, yet there is method in it.* There may be some reason for what appears to be a foolish mistake."

"Rosario . . . Br. Matthew," began Fr. Bill, "think about this for a minute: in almost all kidnappings for ransom, don't the kidnappers normally make direct contact with the victim's family . . . and *only* the victim's family? They don't generally 'go public' . . . as was done here." "Yes," I said, "and very often they warn the family not to tell anyone . . . especially not the authorities." "This is my point," said Fr. Bill, "there's something weird going on here, folks . . . I can feel it in my bones!" "I agree," I said. "Me too." said Rosario.

CHAPTER EIGHT

The next day I couldn't wait to talk with Fr. Bill about Bartolomé de Las Casas. He was on my mind all night long. I couldn't stop thinking about how he went from a complete disregard for the indigenous to becoming their number one advocate and benefactor. I felt a great kinship with him because I, too, held the indigenous in very low esteem and had no interest in their well-being. But in a period of just 24 hours my consciousness had been raised considerably.

After breakfast, Fr. Bill and I sat down in the parlor: "Fr. Bill," I began, "thank you for encouraging me to attend Rosario's presentation last night. I was deeply moved by the generous life of de Las Casas. So much so that I could barely sleep! His life was so beautiful, so rich, so meaningful! And my life, in comparison, was so gross, so empty . . . so meaningless."

"Brother Matthew," responded Fr. Bill, "I'm very happy you went to the presentation! From what Esperanza shared yesterday regarding your attitude toward the indigenous, and given the way the grace of God is at work within you, I thought you might be able to identify with the marvelous life of de Las Casas." "Oh, yes . . . very much so." I replied, "Meditating on his charitable life has caused me to reflect on my own life and to reevaluate it."

"Br. Matthew," began Fr. Bill, "do you remember me mentioning that it seemed to me that St. Augustine wanted to share his life with you by presenting you with his autobiography?" "Yes," I answered. "I think Augustine is trying to help you to do what he did," continued Fr. Bill, "that is . . . to leave behind a decadent, worldly lifestyle. Well, now, it appears that Bartolomé de Las Casas is reaching out to you for the purpose of opening your heart to the poor. So, Augustine is teaching you about true freedom while de Las Casas teaches you about true love. You're on a new path, Br. Matthew, and apparently there are 2 holy souls who have befriended you and have chosen to share their lives with you. That's good news, Brother! The Church calls this friendship . . . this sharing of lives; *the communion of saints*."

"Br. Matthew, if you don't mind, I'd like to digress for a moment," proposed Fr. Bill. "Of course, Fr. Bill." I said. "Br. Matthew . . . what do you think your family and your corporation are doing right now in response to the news of your kidnapping for ransom?" "First of all, Fr. Bill, we already have a policy in place regarding what to do should I ever be kidnapped. The first thing that will happen is that anyone who was with me at the time of the kidnapping will return immediately to our Corporate Headquarters on Park Avenue in Manhattan, NYC. So my pilot, Pancho Luna, is probably on his way back to New York as we speak."

"Next . . . the whole case will be handed over to a team of ransom negotiation experts in London. But I have made it clear to the negotiation firm that they are not to do any negotiating unless they are able to speak with me so as to verify that I am in fact alive and that the people who say they have me actually do have me."

"Ah! Br. Matthew. So that means . . . if the kidnappers want their money, they have to find you!" "Yes," I responded, "and considering that 100 million dollars is worth over a billion Mexican Pesos . . . we can assume they really want the money!" "Therefore," observed Fr. Bill, "chances are they will use all their resources, deploy all their assets, and do everything in their power to find you."

"Good morning, everyone," announced Rosario as she entered the parlor where Fr. Bill and I were sitting: "Have either of you been out yet?" "No," replied Fr. Bill. "Don't even think about it!" exclaimed Rosario, "There are police roadblocks and check points everywhere! It took me twice the amount of time it would normally take to get here this morning because the traffic is backed up for at least a block at every check point. All the roads leading into or out of the city have road blocks, and each and every vehicle is being searched. Also . . . a reward is being offered for any information concerning the whereabouts of Mr. Lake." Fr. Bill glanced over at me and saw the anxiety on my face: "Don't worry, Br. Matthew . . . you will be safe here. Remember; you are not alone . . . you have friends in *really* high places now!"

The next 10 days at the orphanage were filled with new experiences and new insights. They were, without question, 10 of the most wonderful days of my life. I had many long, fruitful conversations with Fr. Bill. He told me there were 3 other Franciscans living in the friary, but all 3 were away for various reasons. Fr. James was in New York City doing fundraising events for the orphanage, and Br. Peter was visiting with his family. Br. Andrew, a psychologist, was attending a seminar in Rome.

Fr. Bill said that he and the other friars were from NY

and were members of the New York province of their community. He said that with the help of Esperanza and Rosario, the friars were actually home-schooling the 12 orphans. Occasionally, they received some help in the form of volunteers from *Casa Na Bolom* (House of The Jaguar); an institute in San Cristobal that was founded in 1951 by the Danish archaeologist, Frans Blom . . . one of the first Europeans to explore the ruins of Palenque. *Casa Na Bolom* is dedicated specifically to helping the Lacandon Maya. Fr. Bill asked me if I might like to teach a little Roman and Greek history to the students . . . perhaps introduce them to the ancient Greek writer, Homer; author of the *Iliad* and the *Odyssey* . . . and to the famous Latin poet, Virgil; author of the *Aeneid*. Naturally, I jumped at the opportunity.

Of course, I had many helpful, spiritual conversations with Fr. Bill as well. I was going through a complete transformation and without Fr. Bill to guide me I don't know how I would have fared. Also, I read the *Confessions* every evening before going to bed and that in itself was like a spiritual direction session with St. Augustine! By that time my beard was pretty full and so, there I was, going about in a Franciscan habit . . . sporting a shaved head and a full beard. When I looked in the mirror I couldn't help but marvel at what the Lord had done with me! If someone had told me on the morning I left the hotel to visit the Cathedral that I would wake the next day in a Franciscan friary with a shaved head, a beard and wearing a Franciscan habit, I would have kept on walking and paid no attention to that individual because I would have assumed the person was mentally disturbed. And yet . . . that is precisely what happened.

One day, I asked Fr. Bill what his thoughts were

regarding how long I should hide out at the orphanage. He said that it would be best to wait until more information emerged regarding the kidnappers. To go to the authorities when we really don't know what's going on could be disastrous. He said that God would show us what to do and when to do it. Reflecting on all the providential things that had happened so far, I knew that what Fr. Bill was suggesting was undoubtedly the best course of action.

A few days later, by the grace of God, the information we had been waiting patiently for surfaced. One of the orphans, a 14-year-old named Carlitos, was returning to the Casa after having gone to the market to purchase some fruit. He was walking down the dead end street and was 3 houses away from the orphanage when he stopped in his tracks to allow a car to turn into a driveway that was directly in front of him. The big driveway gate was being held open by a burly man with long, curly, dark brown hair and wearing a black Tank Top. The gatekeeper had a large tattoo on the upper part of his right arm. It was 2, big, interlocking letters: **L** and **O**. Carlitos felt a chill run down his spine; he knew immediately what the letters signified. They were the initials of... *La Oscuridad*; a new and very aggressive drug cartel that was becoming active in the region.

Carlitos reported that when the black car turned into the driveway and rolled slowly past him it appeared to be the same black Mercedes that was involved in the attempted kidnapping. And since Carlitos was the boy who got the license plate number of the car and had in fact memorized it, he looked at the plate and almost dropped the bag of bananas and guavas he was cradling in his arms; it was definitely the same car used by the kidnappers!

The terrified adolescent said that his heart began pounding so hard he thought it was going to leap out of his chest! After the car passed him and the gate was being closed, he looked straight ahead and continued walking toward the orphanage. And although he was on the verge of exploding with emotion, he adopted a very relaxed stride so as not to reveal the turmoil that had been unleashed within him.

CHAPTER NINE

Later that same day Fr. Bill sat down with me and told me everything Carlitos reported about the kidnappers living only 3 houses away from us. "Fr. Bill," I said . . . my voice trembling as I spoke, "This is unbelievable! The people who tried to kidnap me are only 3 houses away from here? They're our neighbors? Father . . . tell me this isn't happening! Is it possible that Carlitos made a mistake with the license plate number?" "I don't think so," replied Fr. Bill, "considering how terrified and upset Carlitos was by what he saw, I have no problem believing it was the kidnapper's car. Also, Br. Matthew . . . Carlitos said that the gatekeeper bore a striking resemblance to one of the thugs that pursued you into the cathedral. Do you remember one of the men having long hair?"

"Yes!" I answered, "The one that positioned himself behind me so as to cut off my escape . . . he was a brawny fellow with curly, dark brown hair that extended below his ears." "Br. Matthew," said Fr. Bill, "that's the exact description Carlitos gave of the gatekeeper." "But Father," I asked, "don't you know the people on this little block? How could such dangerous people be so close without you knowing anything about it?"

"That particular house, Br. Matthew," began Fr. Bill, "is

a rental. I knew the people who were there previously but they moved out about 4 months ago, and the house was unoccupied for 3 months. The present occupants moved in about a month ago and I haven't met them yet . . . they're extremely private; and now I know why!" "Think about it, Fr. Bill," I said, "I'll bet you they chose that house precisely *because* it's located so close to an orphanage; no one would ever think a cartel would be so bold as to operate out of a house in such a high profile neighborhood. It would be like choosing a house next to a school, a church, or even a police station!"

"I wish you were right, Br. Matthew, but you're thinking as if you're in the USA. Here in Mexico, the cartels set up wherever they want . . . with complete impunity." "I guess I have a lot to learn about Mexico, Fr. Bill." I responded, "But now that we know it was a drug cartel that tried to kidnap me, shouldn't we go to the authorities?" "In the USA," began Fr. Bill, "that would be the logical thing to do. But remember, Br. Matthew, you're not in the USA . . . you're in Mexico! We need more information before we do anything. The Lord is helping us . . . let's just be patient a little longer. That's my suggestion."

"OK, Fr. Bill," I replied, "you know so much more about how things work around here, I'd have to be a complete fool not to follow your advice. Now if you don't mind, Fr. Bill, can you tell me what you know about this group . . . *La Oscuridad*." "Well, Br. Matthew," began Fr. Bill, "here's the thing; nobody really knows anything about them . . . that's one of the reasons for their name; they pride themselves on existing in the shadows . . . in *La Oscuridad!* But it can be assumed that they operate pretty much the same way the other cartels do . . . only with greater stealth and secrecy."

"Maybe this 'secrecy' stuff is the reason they decided to let the indigenous take the blame," I suggested. "That could very well be the case, Br. Matthew," responded Fr. Bill. "But if they really wanted to be secretive, they wouldn't have left any note at all. They simply would have captured you and without identifying themselves or anyone else, contacted your corporation regarding the ransom. Do you see, Br. Matthew? Something is wrong here."

"Yes, Fr. Bill . . . I understand the point you're making." I answered. "There's still a part missing from this puzzle, and until we find that part, nothing is going to make sense." "Precisely, Br. Matthew," responded Fr. Bill . . . as if he was Sherlock Holmes and I was Dr. Watson, "and until we have that missing part to the puzzle, we have to stay put. We're safe behind these walls, Br. Matthew. God has a plan for you . . . and he will show us the way out of this dilemma."

"Fr. Bill," I asked, "you wouldn't happen to have a pair of binoculars, would you? One of the windows in the little chapel on the 2nd floor faces the street. Maybe we can see what's going on at the kidnapper's house." "Excellent idea, Br. Matthew!" replied Fr. Bill, "Yes, I do have a very good pair of binoculars that were given to me by a friend. I use them when I journey out to the missions in the Lacandon Jungle. I'll go get them, and I'll meet you in the chapel in 2 minutes."

Fr. Bill returned to the chapel carrying an antique looking leather case that I presumed contained a pair of very old binoculars. "These, Br. Matthew," began Fr. Bill, "are vintage, World War II, US Army binoculars." "Are you sure they still work, Fr. Bill?" I replied, "When you said a friend gave them to you, I was imagining something a little more, well . . . state-of-the-art!" "They work great, Br. Matthew, you'll see. Now . . . let's take a look at that house." said Fr. Bill.

Fr. Bill crouched down below the window and used the binoculars, which he was already looking through, to lift the curtain from the bottom . . . just enough so he could see out the window. "OK . . . there's the house. Let me focus the lenses a little more . . . good, there we go; perfect! I can see the house, the driveway, the garage and the gate. There are 2 men standing in front of the garage talking. One of them has long hair . . . probably the guy Carlitos described. Yes, it's him . . . I can see the *La Oscuridad* initials on his right arm."

"Is the black Mercedes there, Fr. Bill?" I asked. "I don't see it Br. Matthew." responded Fr. Bill. "Perhaps it's in the garage. Hey . . . hold on! A car is pulling up the driveway and the 2 guys are opening the gate. It's a white Cadillac Escalade. Let's see who this is. OK . . . the guy with the long hair is closing the gate, and the other guy is walking over to the SUV. OK, the driver is coming out of the car . . . he's dressed very professionally, business suit, white shirt and tie; the other guy is shaking his hand . . . now all 3 are standing there talking. Here . . . take a look at this, Br. Matthew."

Fr. Bill passed the binoculars to me and I quickly adjusted the lenses until I could see the 3 men clearly. "I see them, Fr. Bill. These glasses are fantastic!" I exclaimed. "I told you Br. Matthew . . . they were made to last." replied Fr. Bill. "OK . . . here we go, Fr. Bill: the long haired guy is definitely the thug who tried to grab me that day . . . and get this; the other guy is the one who stood in front of me and said he was a Federal Agent! I don't know who the fellow in the suit is because his back is turned toward me. Wait . . . he's answering a call on his cell phone and walking away from the 2 cartel members . . . good, keep going, keep going . . . now turn toward me; Yes! NO, NO! It can't be!" I jerked the binoculars back from the window and just sat there in a daze.

"Br. Matthew . . . what is it? What did you see?" asked Fr. Bill with emotion. "Ricardo Villanueva . . . the Mexican Secretary of Energy." I responded in a dull, zombie-like tone. "Is he the Ricardo you met with the night before the kidnapping attempt?" questioned Fr. Bill. Shaken to the marrow, "Yes" . . . was all I could say.

Fr. Bill turned toward the humble little tabernacle that was on the far wall of the private chapel, blessed himself and thanked Jesus who was present there. "Br. Matthew," began Fr. Bill, "I hope you realize that this information changes everything; this is what we have been waiting for! I know you are in a state of shock after realizing the dastardly way Ricardo betrayed you, but now we know where we stand . . . we know what's going on! We know there is definitely government collusion."

"Fr. Bill," I said, "this was not simply a betrayal . . . this was downright sinister! And this isn't just another case of government collusion with a drug cartel . . . this whole thing was orchestrated from start to finish by the Mexican Secretary of Energy! You see, Fr. Bill, there were certain things said at that meeting in *El Secreto* that I haven't shared with you yet because, up until a few minutes ago, they were irrelevant. But when you hear what those things were, you will see where I'm coming from. First . . . let me ask you this: now that you know Ricardo was in on it, why do you think he organized my kidnapping?"

"Well, Br. Matthew," began Fr. Bill, "it's really quite

obvious: based on what Esperanza said she overheard the two of you discussing that night in the restaurant, about how you wanted to undermine the reputation of the indigenous so that it would be easier to ignore them and drill on their land, Ricardo was already planning to have you kidnapped and to blame it on the indigenous. I suspect that Ricardo was trying to tap into historic fears that Americans have regarding native peoples.

A person in Ricardo's position would be well-versed in American history and would be aware of such things as *The Massacre at Fort William Henry* . . . which had such a devastating effect on the way Americans would come to perceive the indigenous people. Fort William Henry was a British fort on Lake George in upstate New York. The French, with the help of Indians from the locality, took the fort. The Indians were promised some of the 'spoils' . . . which the French never gave them. Consequently, the infuriated Indians began attacking the unarmed British prisoners, killing some and taking others for ransom. This is the kind of fear Ricardo is trying to conjure up. Is that how you see it, Br. Matthew?"

"Yes, Fr. Bill," I replied, "that's exactly how I see it. But what I wanted to share with you was that during that clandestine dinner meeting, Ricardo practically told me I was going to be kidnapped! He said that the indigenous were very bold and would probably do some kind of 'rash act' in the near future. He even asked me if I was ready! And like an idiot, I told him I was born ready! Then, being 100 times more brazen than the meek indigenous, he asked me what my plans were for the next day. And of course, being the naïve fool that I am I told him I was planning to visit the Cathedral."

"Incredible, Br. Matthew . . . just incredible," replied

Fr. Bill, "now I know why you used the word 'sinister' . . . it seems as though he was enjoying deceiving you! It's pathetic to witness the depth of corruption to which some politicians will descend." "It certainly calls to mind," I added, "something Cicero said: *Politicians are not born; they are excreted.*"

"Fr. Bill," I asked, "given the central reason for my kidnapping; that is . . . wanting to make the indigenous look bad; I'm not sure why they included a ransom . . . and an enormous one at that!" "Good question, Br. Matthew," answered Fr. Bill, "I can think of two possible reasons; one being stronger than the other. The first, the weaker of the two, is that a ransom would add to the authenticity and criminal nature of the kidnapping. Remember Brother . . . Ricardo wanted the indigenous to look *really* bad! The second reason is greed . . . pure and simple. A person as morally compromised as Ricardo would never be able to pass up such a rare opportunity to get rich so quickly! The immorality involved doesn't even enter into the picture; money is what he lives for . . . it's what makes him tick!"

"I hate to admit it, Fr. Bill," I confessed, "but the description you just gave of Ricardo fits me very well . . . or at least the person I was before coming to the orphanage. I loved money as much as he does . . . in fact, I was in league with him that evening in the restaurant when we formed a plan to swindle and out-maneuver the poor. Little did I know that the plan we were discussing was my kidnapping!"

"I'm very glad you see it that way, Br. Matthew," said Fr. Bill, "because now you can begin praying for Ricardo, asking the Lord to come to him as he came to you. For all we know, Brother . . . Ricardo could be in Heaven before the two of us! The big mistake many people make, Br.

Matthew, is that they completely overestimate their ability to do what is good and right on their own, without heavenly assistance; while seriously underestimating the weakness of our wounded human nature. They imagine they are self-sufficient and can live a reasonably good life without God's grace or guidance. This Pelagian pride, which has gone viral in today's world, leads one to believe that man is absolutely free and, therefore, there is no need to embrace the objective moral law. Soon, as the conscience is eroded, the line between good and evil becomes dangerously blurred. This is the path you were on and the path Ricardo is on now.

"But," continued Fr. Bill, "thanks be to God . . . humility shows us the way out of this spiritual morass. When we open ourselves to the truth and freely choose to do what we know to be right and good, we become stronger and more likely to initiate even greater works of goodness and righteousness as we continue to grow in grace. The person begins to live from grace to grace . . . that is, the person begins to live a truly spiritual life where they are no longer led astray by worldly desire but are, instead, guided interiorly by the gentle movements and loving inspirations of the Holy Spirit. This is why St. Paul, in Romans 12:21, teaches us to . . . *conquer evil by doing good*. That is the path you are on now, Br. Matthew."

"Well, Br. Matthew," said Fr. Bill, "this has been quite an eventful day . . . to say the least! Why don't we call it a wrap and get a good night's rest. Tomorrow will be a new day, and we can begin afresh with the gifts and blessings that surely await us!" "Sounds good to me," I responded, "¡Hasta mañana!"

CHAPTER TEN

The following morning, after breakfast, Fr. Bill said he wanted to show me something and he asked me to walk with him to the little barn at the back of the property. "Have you ever seen a burro up close, Br. Matthew?" said Fr. Bill as we entered the barn. "No . . . not that I recall, Fr. Bill." I responded. "A burro, Brother, is essentially a donkey; the Spanish word, 'burro' . . . means donkey." continued Fr. Bill. "You know that Jesus, in the fullness of humility, rode into Jerusalem on the back of a donkey. Well, today, Br. Matthew, in humility, you will ride out of San Cristobal de Las Casas with the help of this burro!" "What do you mean, Fr. Bill?" I asked, "I'm not sure I understand you?" "Br. Matthew . . . the time has come for you to leave the orphanage. Now that we know the level of government involvement and the reason for your attempted kidnapping, not to mention the close proximity of the kidnappers, it's much too dangerous for you to stay here."

"Yes, I understand, Fr. Bill," I replied, "and I agree. I gave it a great deal of thought last night and came to the same conclusion. But . . . where will I go? And what does this burro have to do with me leaving San Cristobal?" "The burro belongs to the children and they call him Contento," replied Fr. Bill. "Contento, as you know, is Spanish for 'Happy'. Contento is a wonderful creature; very friendly and very strong. A few of the children get into that little wagon over there and Contento pulls it to various parts of the city, so the children can sell their crucifixes at special events. Sometimes, they recruit Contento to take them to the forest on the outskirts of the city where they collect fruit, berries, and wild chili peppers."

"In about an hour from now, Br. Matthew," continued Fr. Bill, "Contento will be taking you, Antonio, Miguelito and Montecito out to the perimeter of the city." "Yes . . . and then?" I questioned. "Considering how desperate these people are and how intense their search for you will be, Br. Matthew, there's really only one place I can think of where I'm sure you will be safe; the *Montes Azules Biosphere Reserve.* Have you heard of the Reserve, Br. Matthew?" asked Fr. Bill. "Yes, I have, Fr. Bill." I replied. "In fact . . . that's the place I was hoping to get permission to drill in. It's part of the Lacandon Jungle, if I remember correctly."

"Your memory serves you well, Br. Matthew." responded Fr. Bill. "Have you ever been in a jungle, Brother?" "The closest I've ever come to visiting a jungle was when I used to party in *Les Caves du Roy* . . . a famous night club on the French Riviera!" I said with a smile. "OK . . . well, you're in for a wonderful experience, Brother." replied Fr. Bill. "All of the roads in and out of the city now have check points. But Antonio knows a secret way out of the city that the Maya have been using for hundreds of years. It's an ancient trail that I've used many times. It's a little more difficult than the normal route, but with Antonio as your guide you won't have any problem."

"Here's the plan, Br. Matthew," continued Fr. Bill, "the

Montes Azules Reserve is the home of Antonio's people . . . the Lacandon Maya. Antonio will take you to the settlement he calls home; the village of Santa Maria de Guadalupe . . . one of the few Catholic villages in the Reserve. My brother Franciscans and I are responsible for the mission chapel there, and one of us travels out to the village once a month for mass. You will be staying in a little, traditional thatch hut that was built by the local people to be used by missionaries when they come to visit the village. The hut has an earthen floor, a cot, a chair, a table and some shelves. You can take your meals with Antonio and his family. You will be treated very well, Br. Matthew. The people will be extremely happy to have you as their guest!"

"How long will it take to get to the Reserve?" I asked. "All told . . . the journey takes around 6 hours." answered Fr. Bill. "Contento will take you to the village of San Marcos where you and Antonio will meet up with a friend of the orphanage named Mario Puente. This leg of the excursion with Contento will take an hour. Then, using his pickup truck, Mario will take you and Antonio to the Reserve. After a three-hour drive, Mario will drop you off a mile before the official entrance, and Antonio will lead you to Santa Maria by way of a series of interconnecting, jungle trails known only to the local people. That hike through the mountains will take around two hours. You should be in Santa Maria for dinner."

"What about Miguelito, Montecito, and Contento?" I asked. "San Marcos is famous for its mangoes and grapefruit," replied Fr. Bill. "So, Miguelito will load the cart with fruit and head back to the orphanage. That's why I'm sending along the 'Chief of Security,' Montecito; he will guard Miguelito and Contento on the return trip."

"Here's some gas money for Mario," said Fr. Bill, as he handed me a white envelope. "The cook is preparing some food and drinks for your journey. Why don't you get packed now but, remember, you're looking at a two-hour hike through the mountains, so use just one small backpack and take only the bare essentials." "Fr. Bill," I asked, "how long do you think I will need to stay in Santa Maria de Guadalupe?" "I don't know, Brother," replied Fr. Bill, "but once you see how beautiful it is there, you may not want to leave! I will be going to Santa Maria for mass in about a week, and we will have plenty of time to talk and catch up then. Antonio and Miguelito are in the barn getting Contento and the wagon ready, so why don't you meet us in front of the barn in half an hour."

Collecting my things was a rather easy task since everything I brought with me to Mexico was back at the Hotel. The main thing I wanted to be sure to put in my backpack was my Latin copy of the *Confessions*. When I went out to the barn, the little, open wagon was ready to go. Miguelito and Montecito were relaxing in the back and Antonio was upfront sitting on the driver's bench. "Br. Matthew," said Fr. Bill, "here's a hat for you. It will come in handy . . . believe me. Also, it will be an additional help to disguise your true identity. This will be your first time out in public, and we don't want to take any chances. Also, I think it would be best for you to wear this pair of dark sunglasses . . . at least until you are out of the city."

I put on the wide-brimmed, straw hat, along with the sunglasses: "What do think?" I said. "Perfect!" exclaimed Fr. Bill, "Between the Franciscan habit, the glasses, the big hat and the beard . . . no one will ever recognize you! You know, Brother," continued Fr. Bill as he took me aside to speak in private, "when you leave here you are going to pass right in front of the house where the kidnappers are staying. I don't anticipate any problems, but just in case, I will be watching you from the chapel with the binoculars. If you run into any kind of trouble tap the top of your hat with your left hand, and I'll come out to try and help."

"Thanks, Fr. Bill," I said. "Considering how many times you and the boys have passed the house without incident, I'm not at all worried." "Great!" said Fr. Bill. "One last thing, Brother; where you're going is very different than just about any place you've ever been to before. You are going to see and experience things you've never seen or experienced before. You will be living with God's poor . . . in the heart of our Father's creation; it's like the Garden of Eden, Brother! It will take your breath away! Listen to the Lord when you are there; He will speak to your heart through his Spirit."

"I can hardly wait to get there, Fr. Bill!" I exclaimed. "Good!" replied Fr. Bill. "Now let me give all of you a blessing for your journey." Fr. Bill lifted his arms up high toward the heavens and called down the Spirit of God upon us touching each of us, including Montecito and Contento, gently on the head.

Fr. Bill's blessing was so beautiful! As our little wagon expedition rolled out of the orphanage driveway and onto the public street, I felt as though we were surrounded by a cloud of angels and saints! I was surprised at how well the little wagon seemed to be working; we were moving along smoothly and comfortably. Contento was clearly pleased with this opportunity to be out of the barn and to get a little exercise in the open air. Antonio said that Contento knew the way to San Marcos and that he already knew we were going there because Montecito was in the back . . . that was his cue.

As we continued down the block, I kept a wary eye on the third house on the right. We were passing in front of the second house when I heard the screeching sound of a metal gate opening. Antonio, who was driving and sitting on the right side of the bench, nudged me with his left elbow: "Brother!" whispered Antonio, "someone is coming out of the trafficker's house!" "Yes . . . I see him, Antonio. Stay calm." I whispered.

The man stepped onto the sidewalk and lit a cigarette; then he looked up, saw us and waved: "Hey there, Padre, hold on one minute . . . I need to talk with you!" I couldn't believe my eyes! It was the kidnapper with the long hair who had tried to grab me in front of the Cathedral. I told Antonio to stop the wagon . . . and then it dawned on me; the crucifix I was wearing was the same one that this hoodlum had pulled out of my belt, looked at, and threw to the ground. If he saw it . . . he just might remember it!

As the man approached our wagon, using my left hand and blocking his view by raising my right arm . . . which was covered by a more than ample Franciscan habit, I stuffed the crucifix inside my habit. "Padre," began the cartel member as he placed his hands on the edge of the driver's bench . . . just a few inches away from Antonio. Seeing a brutish, strange man approach so close to Antonio, Montecito instantly put his front paws on the back of the driver's bench and hoisted his 150 pounds of muscle and white fur into what was practically a standing position so that he looked like a polar bear balancing upright on its hind legs. He then proceeded to glare directly down at the man he was now towering over and, baring his enormous teeth, gave a ferocious growl that flowed out of his throat like rolling thunder and was so threatening that not only did the man immediately take a step back but Contento himself flinched upon hearing the bloodcurdling snarl.

"It's OK, Montecito!" said Antonio, "you can sit down now . . . it's OK. Good boy, Montecito!" The man, beginning to regain his composure as color returned to his face, glanced at Montecito who was now sitting calmly while Miguelito stroked his soft, white coat. He then continued from where he left off: "Padre . . . I would like to ask a favor of you." "Yes, of course," I responded, "how can I help you?" Antonio turned and just stared at me; the expression on his face was priceless . . . his eyes were like saucers! "Padre . . . I lost something very, very, valuable. Would you please pray to God for me and ask him to help me find it?"

"What was this valuable thing that you lost, my friend?" I asked. "I can't really describe it, Padre. But I can tell you this . . . it was extremely valuable!" "That's OK," I replied, "I already know what it is and you are right . . . it's priceless!" "You know what I lost?" questioned the thug. "If you know what I lost, tell me . . . what did I lose?" "Well . . . it's obvious, my friend. You said that what you lost was exceedingly valuable and you could not describe it; therefore, I think you lost something spiritual. I believe the thing you lost was your *faith*!"

"My faith?" exclaimed the would-be kidnapper. "You're right! I did lose my faith; but that was a long, long time ago . . . and it isn't the thing I'm looking for now." "But," I replied, "perhaps this very valuable thing you are trying to find now is in reality the faith you lost a long time ago. Sometimes we search for spiritual things in the wrong places." "No, Padre," replied the narco-trafficker, "what I'm trying to find is not spiritual . . . it's very physical; it's as real as you sitting there on that bench!" Upon hearing these words, Antonio's eyes rolled back into his head and he almost lost consciousness. "In that case, my friend," I replied, "faith is indeed more valuable than what you lost, because faith is even more real and more authentic than me sitting here on this bench! But why don't we do this: I will ask God to help you find whichever of the two things is in truth the most valuable . . . OK?" "Yes, Padre, that will be fine. Thank you for your prayers." replied the man . . . who was now so confused and dazed he could barely put one foot in front of the other in order to walk back to the 'den of iniquity' from whence he came.

CHAPTER ELEVEN

"**Br. Matthew!**" **exclaimed Antonio,** "I can't believe you spoke the way you did to that criminal! For a minute there, I thought you were just going to come out with it and tell him who you really were; Benjamin Lake, the 'valuable thing' he was looking for!" "Never, Antonio! I'm many things, but suicidal is not one of them. I'm sorry I put you through such a nerve-racking experience, but my instincts told me it would be best to engage that fellow rather than avoid him."

"Antonio?" I asked, "Do you think Montecito would have attacked that man?" "Absolutely, Brother; if that man had grabbed me causing me to scream, Montecito would have pounced on him!" "Wow!" I said. "So, he really is the 'Chief of Security'!" "Oh, yes!" replied Antonio, "His breed is famous for guarding the sheep that live in the mountains of Northern Spain." "Has Montecito ever had to fight off any man or beast?" I asked. "No." answered Antonio, "All he has to do is what you saw him do today, and, so far, that has been enough to scare off any and all threats."

All this time, as we worked our way to the edge of the city, it was obvious that Contento knew exactly where he was going. At one point, to show off Contento's high IQ, Antonio put down the reins and let Contento lead the wagon . . . freestyle. Antonio held his empty hands up in the air: "Look, Brother . . . no hands! You see . . . Contento knows the way better than I do!"

When we finally reached the perimeter of the city Contento took us behind some houses and down a very old, badly broken up, asphalt street that ran between the houses and the forest. After about 100 feet, we made a hard left turn onto a little dirt trail that went directly into the woods. In less than a minute, we were out of the city, immersed in the forest, and completely out of sight.

"Good job, Contento!" said Antonio. "Brother . . . this is the trail that will take us to San Marcos. We should arrive there in about 35 minutes." "Great, Antonio!" I said. "Miguelito . . . Antonio; do you remember in class a few days ago I mentioned a Roman Poet named Virgil?" "Yes." responded the 2 boys. "Do you remember his 3 major Works?" "Yes," answered Antonio, "the *Eclogues,* the *Georgics* . . ." "and the *Aeneid!*" interjected Miguelito with excitement. "Correct! Very good, boys!" I replied. "Well . . . Virgil suggested something in book IX of his first major work, the *Eclogues*, that I think could be of some help to us right now." "Tell us, Br. Matthew! What did Señor Virgil say?" exclaimed Miguelito.

"OK, boys," I began, "this is what he said: *Let us go singing as far as we go; the road will be less tedious.*" "That's a great idea, Br. Matthew!" said Antonio, "but what should we sing?" "Considering how well the good Lord has been watching over us so far on this trip, why not sing . . . *He's got the whole world in His hands!*" "Excellent!" exclaimed Miguelito, "That's one of my favorite songs! Can I be the one to begin it?" "Of course, Miguelito . . . thank you for your enthusiasm!" I answered. And so, Miguelito began to sing:

He's got Mon-te-cito . . . in his hands;
He's got friendly Con-ten-to . . . in his hands;
He's got Mi-gue-lito . . . in his hands;
He's got the whole world in his hands!

"Do you see those houses down there, Brother?" asked Antonio. "That's San Marcos." Antonio was pointing to a small village tucked away in a cozy, little valley. When we arrived in San Marcos, we went directly to Mario Puente's house and within ten minutes, after saying "Adios" to Miguelito, Montecito, and Contento, we were on our way to the world famous . . . *Montes Azules Biosphere Reserve.*

"Tell me, Br. Matthew," said Mario as we drove along the road that leads to the Lacandon Jungle, "have you ever been to the *Montes Azules Biosphere Reserve?*" "No, Mario," I replied, "have you been there?" "Yes, Brother," answered Mario, "I was born there!" Mario was a middle-aged man and, like Antonio, a Lacandon Maya. "It's very beautiful, Brother . . . you will like it there!" declared Mario. "What village are you going to?" inquired Mario. "I'm going to Antonio's village," I replied. "Oh! Then you are going to the village of *Santa Maria de Guadalupe* . . . that's my village also!" exclaimed Mario.

"Speaking of Santa Maria," said Antonio, "why don't we pray the Holy Rosary together, like we do when we make this trip with Fr. Bill. We can ask *La Virgencita* to protect us and escort us safely to our destination." "I like that idea very much, Antonio!" I said. "Yes . . . me, too!" added Mario, "We need to ask *La Morenita* ("The brown skinned girl" . . . Our Lady of Guadalupe) to watch over my truck; I've been having some problems with it recently." "How old is your truck, Mario?" I asked. "Well, Br. Matthew, it's not really that old; 50 years is old . . . and my truck is only

41 years old!" "Wow! In that case, Mario," I said in a state of shock, "I'm not going to ask you how many miles are on it!" "Too many, Br. Matthew . . . way too many!" replied Mario.

During our 3-hour trip, Mario took the opportunity to give me a little background regarding the *Montes Azules Biosphere Reserve*. He said it was established in 1978 as Mexico's first biosphere reserve and was financed in 1992 by the *World Bank's Global Environmental Fund*. The *United Nations Environment Program* recognizes the Reserve for its global biological and cultural significance.

Mario went on to say that, because of the Reserve's size and biodiversity, *Conservation International*, a Washington, DC-based environmental group, designated it as a "biodiversity hotspot". He said the Biosphere was home to many endangered species, such as the red macaw, the tapir, the spider monkey and the swamp crocodile. It is also home to the 3rd largest big cat in the world . . . the Jaguar; the largest cat in the Americas.

As Mario shared all this fantastic information about his homeland, it was quite obvious that he was very proud of the natural beauty and overall importance of the *Montes Azules*. At the time, however, I can't say I was all that impressed with his description of the Reserve. It's not that I didn't have a sense of aesthetics. It's just that I didn't appreciate sufficiently or properly the value and significance of nature; I didn't understand how precious it is. And I certainly didn't see it as a gift!

But thanks to Augustine, de Las Casas, Fr. Bill, and the poor, I was well on my way to a much needed personal and spiritual renewal. I was beginning to recognize how blind I was with regard to the poor and the natural environment. By the grace of God, my heart and mind were opening so that I could honestly admit the crass insensitivity of my former lifestyle; a way of living in which I moved, not from grace to grace . . . but from greed to greed!

"Br. Matthew," asked Antonio, "did Fr. Bill tell you what happened to my parents?" "No, Antonio." I responded. "My mother died giving birth to me, and 7 years later my father died from a ruptured appendix; they couldn't get him to the hospital in time." "I'm very sorry, Antonio," I said, "I'm sure you miss them very much." "Yes . . . I do miss them." replied Antonio, "But God has given me a beautiful new family at the orphanage. When we get to my village, you will meet my grandparents from my father's side. They are very generous and will share everything they have with you. My abuela (grandmother) makes the most delicious corn tortillas . . . you will love them!" "I'm sure I will, Antonio." I replied, "I'm looking forward to meeting your grandparents, Antonio. Do they speak Spanish?"

"Yes, Brother," answered Antonio, "you will be able to speak with them. My grandfather, Raul, is a spiritual man. You will enjoy him and he will enjoy you!" "Will we be having dinner with your grandparents tonight, Antonio?" I asked. "Yes, Brother," answered Antonio. "My grandparents have a deep appreciation for wisdom . . . but they can't read. Did you bring your Latin copy of the *Confessions* with you, Brother?" "Yes, Antonio . . . I certainly did." I responded. "Brother, if it isn't too much trouble, do you think tonight after dinner you could read a little of the *Confessions* to my grandparents? They would be so happy if you would share some of the knowledge contained in that book with them! Fr. Bill always reads for them after he has dinner at their house." "Of course, Antonio," I replied. "Sounds like a plan to me . . . and a great one at that! Maybe what we can do, if your grandparents would enjoy it, is this: I will read a passage from the book and then we can discuss what was read." "That would be wonderful, Brother!" exclaimed Antonio. "You are very innovative, Br. Matthew . . . never before have we followed up the reading with a discussion. My grandparents are going to love it! You are going to be famous in the village of *Santa Maria de Guadalupe*, Br. Matthew!"

"I'm glad you like the idea, Antonio," I said, "and I'm especially happy you think my idea will be well received by your grandparents. I certainly don't want to come into *Santa Maria* like a bull in a china shop!" "I can assure you, Brother," said Antonio, "you will not offend anyone. On the contrary; the people will see how much you love them because they know how difficult it is, especially for a foreigner, to come to *Santa Maria* . . . and yet, you were willing to make that sacrifice in order to visit with them."

"OK, Br. Matthew," announced Mario, "we're just about there. Another mile or so and we'll reach the trailhead that leads to the village of *Santa Maria de Guadalupe*."

CHAPTER TWELVE

"That's the trail?" I exclaimed, "It hardly looks like a trail to me. All I see is a small space between 2 big bushes. Are you sure that's the trail?" "Yes, Brother," answered Mario, "it's a little overgrown right now . . . but that's why I gave each of you a machete. Don't worry . . . it opens up once you get a little further into it." "Wow . . . no sign or anything. How would anyone ever find it?" I asked.

"When it's the path that leads home," answered Mario, "somehow, a person will find it . . . no matter how hidden it might seem to be." "That's a beautiful thought, Mario." I said. "You've given me something wonderful to reflect on as we journey along this mysterious trail." "You will find, Brother," said Mario, "that the mountains, the forest and the simple, Mayan way of life offer many opportunities for reflection."

Truer words were never spoken . . . at least as far as I was concerned. The minute we got "off the beaten path" and entered upon the trail that led to who knows where . . . it was as if I entered into a new world; a world that was created specifically for reflection and contemplation. I immediately began to reflect on the theme Mario gave me, *the path that leads home.*

Was I, from an existential point of view, on the path

that leads home? Fr. Bill had told me many times that I was on a new path and he indicated that this was the path that would lead me to where God wanted me. As a person, I was changing dramatically. The way I thought and felt about life, the way I valued things, my priorities and such, all of this was in the process of being awakened and completely transformed.

Practically speaking, the trail I was traversing with Antonio led to a place I knew nothing about. In fact, if something had happened to Antonio I would have been utterly lost in the heart of the Lacandon Jungle. And yet, there I was . . . following a Mayan teenager into, what was for me, a total mystery! Is this how a person goes home? Maybe so! And then I remembered what Jesus said about how a person must lose his life in order to find it. And, I thought, wasn't that in essence what Mario was hinting at when, in describing the path home, he said: *somehow, a person will find it . . . no matter how hidden it might seem to be.*

And then I began to reflect on the Mayan people I had come to know: Rosario, Antonio, and Mario. How could I begin to understand their marvelously intuitive nature and their ability to grasp immediately deeply spiritual concepts and realities? I had never seen anything like it. I knew that Alexander the Great was taught by Aristotle . . . but it almost seemed as if the Mayan people had Socrates himself as their tutor (Socrates taught Plato and Plato taught Aristotle)! What would it be like to live in a village full of these uniquely thoughtful and spiritual people?

"Br. Matthew," called Antonio, "could you come here? I want to show you something." Antonio had been leading the way and I was about 20 feet behind him. "Yes, Antonio . . . what is it?" I responded as I hurried to his side. "I want to show you why you must never leave the trail," began Antonio. "Stand right here and don't move an inch." Antonio took a few steps, a distance of maybe 6 feet, and using his machete pointed to the ground directly in front of him: "looks like perfectly solid ground, doesn't it Brother?" "Yes . . . it certainly does, Antonio." I replied. "Watch!" said Antonio. Then, using his machete, he began to hack the vines, and small plants that covered the ground.

In less than 5 seconds, with only 3 or 4 blows from his machete, an enormous hole in the ground was revealed. It was around 6 feet in diameter and at least 15 feet deep. "This is a pit-cave, brother," said Antonio. "'they're all over the jungle. This is one of the reasons why we have a system of reliable trails that have been in use for centuries." "Wow, Antonio!" I exclaimed, "Thanks so much for showing me this. I have already been tempted a number of times to step off the trail and look at something that caught my attention. I'm glad I didn't give way to my curiosity!" I know this trail very well, Brother," said Antonio, "and this is the only pit that is close to the trail so you would have been OK. But I can assure you, Brother . . . there are many other good reasons why you should stay on the trail, and you will learn about them in due time."

"Antonio . . . it's amazing!" I exclaimed, "You just gave me the follow up theme I can reflect on for the remainder of our hike: *good reasons to stay on the path home!*" "I'm glad you are enjoying the hike, Brother," replied Antonio, "We will reach Santa Maria in less than an hour. When we get to the village, I will take you to the mission house and you can rest a little before dinner. Do you mind, Brother, if my grandparents invite some friends and relatives to dinner? When I tell them you are going to read and then follow up the reading with a discussion, they will want to share this rare opportunity with others."

"No . . . I don't mind at all, Antonio," I answered, "What a beautiful idea! It would be a great way for me to meet some of the people of Santa Maria." "Brother . . . did Fr. Bill tell you what he does when he visits Santa Maria?" asked Antonio. "All he told me, Antonio," I answered, "was that he visits the village to celebrate mass." "Yes," replied Antonio, "he celebrates the holy mass . . . but he also visits various families that are struggling in one way or another. Sometimes, a family will come to the mission house to visit the missionary. I'm just telling you this, Brother, because I suspect the people will be expecting you to do the same thing. If you don't want to do it you don't have to. You could just say that you are tired and need to rest."

"Oh no, Antonio . . . I do want to do it!" I exclaimed. "What better way to spend my time in the village than visiting with the people. "This is great, Brother!" exclaimed Antonio, "The people will be so happy to meet with you! You have no idea how much this type of visit means to the people. When you come to see them, they will feel as if Jesus himself is visiting with them!"

When Antonio said this, all I could think of was . . . what would the people think if they knew who I really was? Benjamin Lake . . . the greedy, heartless billionaire who was ready and willing to drive them out of their homes and destroy their precious environment just so that I could make some money . . . money that I definitely did *not* need! And to think that people of my ilk look upon the poor, and especially the indigenous, as lacking in the social graces, in refinement, education and even in morality. What hypocrites we are! What could be less graceful, refined, intelligent, or moral than what I had been preparing to do to them?

Besides . . . even if they did lack refinement, according to some unreasonably applied standard, I would prefer to have that deficit than to be downright evil . . . which is what I was! I began to reflect on my life; when did money become an idol for me? How did I become so cold and heartless, so selfish and insensitive . . . so indifferent to those in need? I was already halfway out the door when I allowed my interior life to disintegrate into a foolhardy attempt to "serve two masters" *(Matthew 6:24)*. Lost and lacking direction because of a compromised moral compass, I was vulnerable . . . and it was just a matter of time before I fell. I don't remember consciously choosing evil . . . but I *do* remember turning away from God. So, with the traumatic death of my parents, I went sailing out the door altogether . . . and slammed it behind me! Nevertheless, by the merciful grace of God, there I was; journeying back home . . . and being led by a child. *(Isaiah 11:6)*

As we hiked along, deeper and deeper into the jungle, it was as though I had passed "through the looking glass" into a new and exotic world . . . replete with marvels of every sort! "Brother," called Antonio, "look at those beautiful yellow and purple flowers over there." "Yes, Antonio," I answered, "I see them . . . they're marvelous!" "We Mayans," continued Antonio, "believe that flowers are one of the ways that God tells us he loves us." "I knew it!" I thought to myself, "We did pass through Lewis Carroll's looking glass and have entered into his famous *Garden of Live Flowers* . . . where the flowers can speak. The difference, however, is that this Elysium is even more enchanted than Alice's Wonderland; here, not only can the flowers speak . . . but they speak for God; they communicate a *spiritual* message!"

Antonio stopped and waited for me to catch up to him: "Look up there, Brother," said Antonio as he pointed to a branch in a nearby tree, "Do you see that brightly colored bird with the big, orange bill?" "Yes! I see it, Antonio. It's incredible! What kind of bird is it?" I asked, filled with excitement. "That's a Toucan," replied Antonio, "You will come to discover, Brother, that my people have a great appreciation for birds. We love to hear them singing because we feel that their songs are meant to teach us about the beauty of heaven!"

"You have a beautiful relationship with God's creation, Antonio." I said, "I'm afraid my relationship with nature is . . . well, let's just say it's in serious need of development; and for sure, that would be an understatement!" "Maybe," replied Antonio, "that's the very reason God is leading you to visit with my people in the *Montes Azules*. The Bible says that God has a special place in his heart for orphans, widows, and strangers. You're not a widow . . . but you've got the other two covered!" "You're right, Antonio," I answered, "I'm an orphan, and I am certainly a stranger to these beautiful mountains and the people of Santa Maria de Guadalupe."

CHAPTER THIRTEEN

Sometimes the trail was around 15 feet wide and fairly level . . . making the hiking relatively easy. Other times, the trail was quite narrow . . . 5 feet at best . . . and very steep, rocky and long; say . . . the length of a football field. Those sections were tough. At one point, as we were ascending one of those treacherous, steep sections, we passed 2 Mayan women coming down the trail with a group of small children. All of them were barefoot . . . and they negotiated the damp, slippery trail so well you would have thought they were out for a pleasant, Sunday afternoon promenade on the *Champs-Élysées* in Paris!

After approximately 2 hours, we came to yet another one of those steep, narrow sections of which I was not very fond. "Br. Matthew," called out Antonio, "we are almost there. When we reach the top of this hill, we will be in my village!" "I'm real glad to hear that, Antonio!" I exclaimed. "I'm looking forward to turning on the fan and collapsing on the cot at the mission house." "Brother," said Antonio, "I hate to disappoint you, but there is no electricity in Santa Maria." "Oh . . . eh . . . yeah . . . of course; Fr. Bill said the mission house was a thatch hut. But there is plumbing and running water . . . right?" "No, Brother," replied Antonio, "we use outhouses, and we drink rainwater."

"OK," I said, trying to stay positive, "nothing wrong with a little rainwater every once in a while. And as for outhouses . . . some rural homesteads in the United States still use them. I'll be fine." "You're going to love my village, Brother," replied Antonio, "the Holy Virgin of Guadalupe and St. Juan Diego will watch over you!" "Who is St. Juan Diego?" I asked. "He's the patron saint of indigenous people," answered Antonio. "He's the indigenous man the Mother of God chose to be her messenger. She sent him to ask Bishop Zumárraga to build a shrine on the hill called Tepeyac." "OK . . . I remember now," I said, "He's the one who had the image of Mary miraculously imprinted on his poncho." "On his *tilma*, Brother!" added Antonio.

We finally reached the top of the hill and stopped to catch our breath. After we had rested for around 5 minutes Antonio said: "We made it, Brother. We are here . . . this is the village of Santa Maria de Guadalupe." I looked around: "All I see is rainforest, Antonio . . . where's the village?" He pointed to a little trail maybe 3 feet wide: "Follow me!" he said.

We trudged along that miniscule trail for about 30 feet and then, lo and behold . . . spread out before us in a serene mountain dale was the picturesque, Mayan village of Santa Maria de Guadalupe. "Wow, Antonio," I proclaimed, "your village is so completely traditional! Every dwelling is made out of natural materials. I was expecting to see more houses of cement block." "Brother," replied Antonio, "who is going to carry hundreds of cement blocks up the steep, dangerous slopes we just traversed?" "Not me . . . that's for sure, Antonio!" I declared. "The walls of the houses are made of branches that are trimmed and tied together," explained Antonio,

"And the roofs are composed of many layers of palm fronds. My people developed a special way of arranging them that has been in use for hundreds of years. You will see, Brother; even with the hardest downpours . . . there is very little leakage."

"Amazing, Antonio!" I replied, "I can see already that this is going to be an extremely interesting experience!" "You can count on it, Brother!" said Antonio, "You will experience God here!" "That's exactly what Fr. Bill told me, Antonio." I replied. "What about you, Antonio . . . what's it like for you when you are back in your village?" "I feel very close to God when I am here, Brother. I sense the mysterious presence of Juan Diego and the Holy Virgin. Come, Brother . . . I will lead you to the mission house so you can rest before dinner."

We walked through the center of the village on the main, dirt pathway, en route to the mission house . . . which was attached to the mission chapel by a *Swiss Family Robinson* style open breezeway. I was struck by the fact that I only saw 2 or 3 people, a few dogs, some chickens, a couple of burros and a pig. "Where is everyone, Antonio?" I inquired, "This is like a ghost town!" "Oh . . . they're around, Brother. They try to escape the heat as much as possible; so they are either in the forest working or in their homes relaxing."

"Well then," I said, "I think I'm already becoming enculturated because that's exactly what I'm planning on doing . . . relaxing!" "Do you see that house up ahead with the cross attached to the peak, Brother?" questioned Antonio, "That's the chapel; the structure just to the right of it is where you will be staying. I will come and get you when dinner is ready and my grandparent's home is only a short walk from the mission house. Don't forget to bring your book, Brother." "I won't, Antonio," I replied, "I'm really looking forward to this evening." "Do you know what section you're going to read?" asked Antonio. "No . . . not yet, Antonio." I answered, "I guess I'll choose something appropriate after dinner." "Great, Brother . . . I can't wait!" exclaimed Antonio.

The mission house was just as Fr. Bill had described it. The canvas cot had a white sheet, a blanket, and a pillow. The little desk had a bible on it. The unfinished, wooden bookshelf next to the desk held a number of interesting things; there was a book about St. Juan Diego and another told the story of Bartolomé de Las Casas. A couple of books on St. Francis, a manual outlining the Mayan language, and a directory listing all the plants and animals present in the Reserve completed the little jungle library. Also kept there were useful items such as mosquito repellant, candles, and matches that were stored in a moisture proof, plastic container.

I collapsed on the cot and stared at the thatch ceiling. "How can a roof consisting of palm leaves keep out the rain?" I thought to myself. It was obvious that it did because the earthen floor was as dry as a bone. The small lizards that were dashing in and out of the multiple layers of palm seemed to enjoy the protection the roof provided them as well. But keeping out the rain, while clearly an enormously important accomplishment, was trivial compared to the new threat facing the people which, if it were not kept out, would mean the end of their traditional, natural lifestyle. No amount of thatch would be sufficient to keep out a cold-hearted, greedy oil company!

With this type of reflection, I could see that the natural beauty of the rainforest combined with the simplicity of Mayan culture was already turning me into a contemplative. My mind was relaxing and my thoughts were settling into a deeper place in my heart. I could feel my soul expanding and my interior freedom being restored. "If San Cristobal is called, *'the most magical of the magical villages'* . . . what would be an appropriate, honorific title for a place as wondrous as Santa Maria de Guadalupe?" I thought to myself. As I contemplated this question, I fell into a deep, peaceful sleep.

"Wake up, Brother Matthew. It's Antonio . . . it's time for dinner, Brother." announced Antonio, gently, as he tapped on the mission house door. "I'm on my way, Antonio." I replied as I rose from my cot, still fully dressed . . . shoes and all! The sun was setting and hundreds of birds were chirping furiously as they positioned themselves in the countless trees that surrounded the village; each bird hoping to get as good and as safe a spot as possible for the long night's rest that would soon begin.

The village was much more alive now than when we had arrived. We passed about 5 houses and saw quite a few people at each house. Antonio greeted the people as we walked by and many of the people welcomed me . . . even though they weren't sure who I was: "Hola, Padre . . . bienvenidos!" (Hello, Father . . . welcome!), they called out, recognizing the Franciscan habit. It was dinnertime and everyone was returning to their homes from their various chores and activities. The sweet aroma of wood burning fires filled the air.

"This is my grandparent's house, Brother." declared Antonio, proudly. His grandmother, Monica, was in front of the house cooking over an outdoor fire pit. We greeted her, went inside and were met by Antonio's grandfather, Raul, and 4 other relatives. After a few friendly words were exchanged, the food began arriving on the simple wooden table and, in order to "get it while it's hot," we began eating immediately.

For at least an hour, we feasted on the most delicious *frijoles y arroz con pollo* (beans and rice with chicken) I have ever had! Antonio was right; the fresh, hot, homemade corn tortillas were beyond description! For dessert, we had a bowl of fresh banana and papaya pieces topped with a little wild honey. It wasn't *El Restaurante Lum* in the Hotel Bo . . . it was better! The simplicity, humility, and sincerity of the hosts was absolutely disarming. Never had I experienced such hospitality. I felt as though I was truly a member of their family. In Mexico, there is a saying that is widely known: *Mi casa es su casa* (My house is your house). In the USA, due to the aggressive individualism that is rampant, the mentality is more like this: *Mi casa es mi casa . . . y su casa es mi casa tambien!* (My house is my house . . . and your house is my house also!)

But in Santa Maria de Guadalupe, the spirit of hospitality goes way beyond the simple but laudable act of sharing one's home with a visitor. In Santa Maria, the home was not considered to be relevant . . . or at least not to be of primary importance. The "vibes" I picked up from Antonio's family was that they were telling me that . . . *now, because God has sent you to visit with us: we belong to you and you belong to us.* In other words, they wanted to share their *lives* . . . not just their home.

I was so moved by this innocent expression of authentic love that I thought for a moment I might be overcome with emotion and find myself in the uncomfortable position of having to make a scene by wiping the tears from my eyes. At the same time, though, I could sense that even if I had been moved to tears, it would not have been perceived in a negative way. Surprisingly, just the opposite happened; I found myself brimming with a profound joy that emerged mysteriously from some unknown place within me. But how could this be? The incident reminded me of the remarkable, but perplexing, experience I had with Rosario when we were visiting the churches in San Cristobal.

After dinner, Antonio set up a chair for me a little distance away from the table: "This is where Fr. Bill sits when he reads to us. Are you ready, Brother?" asked Antonio. "Almost, Antonio . . . almost; is anyone else coming?" I asked. "Yes . . . 5 other people are coming. They should be here any minute now." answered Antonio. "Great! I guess we will have a full house." I proclaimed. "Not really, Brother," replied Antonio. "Fr. Bill usually has around 20 people. You will probably have 20 tomorrow night."

I reached for my Latin copy of St. Augustine's *Confessions* and opened it hoping to find something appropriate to share with my little "congregation": "What's this?" I mumbled in a low voice. "What book is this? This is English! This isn't the *Confessions!*" I quickly flipped to the cover: *"The Little Flowers of St. Francis?* A book I never heard of. How did that happen?" Upon rising from my "power-nap," I must not have been completely awake and ended up grabbing the wrong book. As the old saying goes; man proposes and God disposes.

I turned back to the page I had originally opened to. It was chapter XXVI: *How St. Francis converted certain robbers and assassins . . . who became friars.* That sounded interesting enough and so, without further ado, I began to read: *"At that time there were 3 famous robbers in that part of the country, who did much evil in all the neighborhood."* The story went on to relate how a certain friar refused to give a group of robbers some food when they came to his door begging. St. Francis arrived at the house shortly thereafter, carrying a small sack of bread and wine which he had received while begging, and reproved the friar for failing to give food to the robbers simply because they were sinners.

Francis then handed the friar the provisions he had just procured and told him to go in search of the men he turned away and, after begging their forgiveness, give them the bread and wine. The friar was instructed to invite the men to turn from their destructive lifestyle and come and live with the Franciscans where all of their needs would be taken care of. The criminals were so impressed with the love and humility of the friar that they accepted his invitation and embarked on a completely new life as Franciscans.

As I read the story to the group I could not escape the feeling that this story was meant more for me than for them. Wasn't I, perhaps in some indirect sense . . . a robber and a murderer? How many innocent people had lost money, and in some cases, maybe even their lives, because of the inconsiderate, heartless business deals for which I was responsible? And, up until just a few weeks ago, wouldn't I have displaced these beautiful people sitting in front of me without giving it a second thought? Sure, I would have! I would have taken the eyes out of their heads and told them they could see better without them! No question about it . . . I was as self-serving and rapacious as the brigands in the story . . . if not more so; the property I took from others I had no need of; it was pure, unmitigated greed!

My audience loved the grand finale . . . when the

bandits became Franciscans. They all smiled and a few sighed with wonder. Monica could not resist giving a gentle applause. One of the young adults present, tapping into the cheerfulness of the moment, asked me if I had been a *ladron* (robber) before becoming a Franciscan. Given the playful mood of the group, I knew that no one would believe me, so I told the truth and said that I had in fact been a swindler but now, as a Franciscan, I beg from those who have . . . so that I can give to those who have not! Everyone burst out laughing. Apparently, being immersed in Mayan culture had not affected in the least my talent for making a quick recovery!

But the truth was inescapable; although the listeners thoroughly enjoyed the reading, the story held special meaning for me, and it spoke to my heart in a very profound way. Antonio gave me a signal indicating that the reading was a great success and that it was now time to begin the discussion. This turned out to be most interesting. The Mayan people are by nature more inclined to listen than to speak . . . and I had observed this wonderful trait at the orphanage. But I was concerned that this attitude would work against a vibrant, open discussion. What I discovered was quite unexpected.

I started the discussion by asking the listeners if they enjoyed the story. Some responded with a nod of the head indicating that they did enjoy it, while others simply said, "Si" . . . (Yes). Then I asked: "What part of the story did you like the most?" Antonio raised his hand as if he was in a classroom. "Yes, Antonio," I said. "I liked the part where they were moved to turn away from evil and live a good life!" declared Antonio. "Yes . . . I liked that part, too." I said.

The fact that Antonio was participating in the

discussion didn't say much because, being a student, he was accustomed to this type of exchange. After Antonio spoke, however, there was a deafening silence for about 2 minutes and, believe me . . . in that particular context, 2 minutes seemed like an eternity! I was considering ending the "discussion" when Raul began to speak: "Br. Matthew, thank you so much for visiting with us this evening and for sharing that beautiful story . . . I enjoyed the story immensely! The part of the story that touched my heart most deeply was the profound concern that St. Francis showed for the souls of those evil men; he felt entirely responsible for them. So much so that he was willing to go hungry in order that he might possibly lead them to salvation. It reminded me of what Jesus said to his disciples in John 4:32, when they were insisting that he eat something but instead he shared with them his concern for the salvation of the Samaritan woman: *I have food you know not of.*"

I could not believe what I had just heard! I felt like one of the people in Jesus' hometown who said of Jesus: *Where did he get all this wisdom? Is this not the carpenter's son?* (Matthew 13: 54-55). Was Raul not a Mayan who was born and raised in the Lacandon rainforest? How could someone who has lived in a thatch hut with an earthen floor his whole life respond as he did? I would have expected a reflection such as his to come forth from the mind and heart of, say . . . one of the Jesuits stationed at St. Ignatius Loyola Church on the Upper East Side of Manhattan; a church my family used to visit from time to time when I was a boy.

After Raul shared, there was about a minute of silence, then a younger man named Juan, who appeared to be in his late twenties, began to speak: "The story reminded me of the time St. Francis tamed the wolf who was terrorizing the town of Gubbio. St. Francis' peace and love saved not only the wolf but the townspeople as well! The same sort of 'radiation of the good' took place in the story you just read to us. The conversion of the robbers was not only good for them . . . it was also a blessing for everyone who lived in that area. It shows us how a single act of charity can quickly become 'good news' for countless people!"

"This isn't really happening!" I thought to myself. "As if Raul's reflection wasn't spectacular enough, now I have a second spiritual virtuoso in my little group!" Again . . . there was a long, minute and a half pause and then a young woman named Carmen began to share. She was very soft spoken and I had to strain at times to hear her: "What I observed in the story, Br. Matthew, was how focused St. Francis was on sanctity. His concern for the outlaw's souls was total; he was determined to bring them to holiness! He knew full well that we are all made for, and called to . . . holiness; that to be one with God is our primary vocation in this life. It was beautiful to see how, because of Francis' deep faith in holiness, he actually facilitated its development in those most unlikely candidates!"

Having witnessed Carmen's brilliant contribution to the discussion, it was now clear that the deep spirituality of Raul and Juan was not some sort of an anomaly but that this was in fact a village full of spiritual masters! Following Carmen, there was a 5-minute pause. We just sat there in the soft glow of candlelight . . . listening to the mysterious sounds emanating from the rainforest. Then Antonio, by making the sign of the cross in a very discreet way, signaled to me that I should end the meeting with a prayer.

The only prayer I could remember was the Lord's Prayer. And so . . . I closed the book, sat up straight, and began: "Padre Nuestro . . ." (Our Father).

CHAPTER FOURTEEN

The following morning I made my way over to Antonio's grandfather's house for breakfast. Raul, Monica, and Antonio were there enjoying some breakfast tacos made with scrambled eggs and refried beans. "Buenos Dias, Br. Matthew. Come and join us; would you like a cup of coffee?" offered Monica. "Are you hungry, brother?" asked Raul, "We have some delicious breakfast tacos for you!" "Yes . . . thank you . . . I am hungry." I replied. "Did you sleep well, Brother?" asked Antonio. "Like a baby, Antonio!" I responded.

"After breakfast, if you would like, Brother, we can begin visiting the people." began Antonio. "Sure . . . that sounds great, Antonio." I replied. "The first house I think you should visit is the home of a 10-year-old boy who was bitten by a venomous snake 6 months ago and is still sick in bed and unable to walk." said Antonio. "Wow, Antonio, that seems like a long time to be disabled from a snake bite!" I exclaimed. "Yes, Brother, it is." responded Antonio.

"You see, Brother" explained Antonio, "this particular case is more complicated than a normal snake bite. The boy's name is Gustavo, but he is affectionately known as Tavito. Tavito and his little, 8-year-old brother, Cuitlahuac, everyone calls him Cuit (pronounced, *Queet*), went into the forest to gather firewood. When Tavito picked up some dead branches, he was bitten on his left index finger by a small, but deadly venomous snake. We are trained from a very early age, Brother, regarding what to do in order to survive such an incident. Tavito immediately placed his bleeding finger on a log and ordered his little brother to hack off the wounded finger using one solid stroke of the machete."

"You can't be serious, Antonio!" I exclaimed. "Did Cuit actually chop off his brother's finger?" "Yes!" answered Antonio, "He had to . . . or his brother would have died." "What a traumatic experience for both of them, Antonio!" "It was horrible, Brother, but now the village looks upon little Cuit as a hero; everyone tells him that if he did not have the strength and the courage to do what he did . . . Tavito would have died. The villagers want to remind him that he did something good . . . he saved a life! Because when someone does something like that, very often they go through life feeling guilty for having maimed a loved one."

"Let's go see Tavito, Antonio," I said, "do you think Cuit will be there?" "Yes . . . he will be there." answered Antonio, "Cuit helps his brother with everything." Antonio went on to tell me that a big problem for the villagers is that the closest hospital is in San Cristobal which is approximately 5 hours away. Many people, including Antonio's own father, have died for this reason. And that was also the reason why Tavito was still in such a debilitated state. The village leaders had been asking for the construction of small clinics closer to where the people live . . . but nothing was ever done to address the problem.

When we arrived, the two brothers were in the house alone; apparently, the parents were in the fields tending to their crop of beans and corn. Tavito was lying on a little cot with Cuit sitting nearby on a wooden stool. "Hello . . . my name is Br. Matthew; how are you feeling today Tavito?" I asked. "I feel OK, Brother . . . but I don't have any strength." answered Tavito. "I understand, Tavito." I said, "God has strength, Tavito . . . and he will share it with you when the time is right. I know because he did it with me once. Be patient . . . you will get better." The house was dark and musty. I asked Tavito if he could walk and he said he was too weak. "Do you ever go outside to enjoy the sunshine?" I asked. "No," responded Tavito. "It's a very beautiful day; would you like to go outside?" I inquired. "Yes!" replied Tavito with enthusiasm, "But how . . . I can't walk?"

"We will carry you on your cot!" I replied. I instructed Antonio and Cuit to pick up one end of the cot while I picked up the heavy end. Then together, we carried Tavito out into the sunshine and the fresh air. "¡Gracias! ¡Estoy muy feliz aqui!" ("Thank you! I am very happy here!) exclaimed Tavito. He was clearly elated to be seeing once again the glorious, tall trees of the forest . . . along with an array of colorful birds and beautiful flowers; and, in the distance, the majestic mountain peaks that encompassed the peaceful, high valley.

As we relaxed and admired the grand display of natural beauty that surrounded us, Tavito noticed something: "Is that a lamb I hear?" "Yes," answered Cuit, "our neighbor received him as a gift just yesterday." "I would love to see him!" responded Tavito, "Where is he . . . I can't see him?" The lamb was only about 20 yards away . . . but there were a number of bushes between us and his location. "Tavito, if you want to see the lamb, you will have to walk; it's too far to carry you. Antonio and I will help you . . . do you want to give it a try? It sounds to me like the lamb is calling you. I think he wants to meet you!"

"Yes . . . I'm sure he does want to meet me!" exclaimed Tavito, "Come on . . . help me up; let's go see the little lamb." Tavito positioned himself on the cot so that he was sitting with his legs over the side and his feet on the ground. Antonio and I then sat next to him, me on one side and Antonio on the other. "On the count of three, Tavito . . . up you go. Ready?" I asked. "Yes." replied Tavito. "One . . . Two . . . Three!" In what seemed like a flash . . . all 3 of us were on our feet and walking toward the lamb.

Little Cuit was in front of us acting like a combination guide/cheerleader: "You're walking Tavito! You're doing great! This way . . . over here; a little to the right now. Easy does it . . . you're almost there." When we reached the small, homemade corral where the lamb was kept, I told Tavito to hold on to the wooden rail: "Do you think you can stand here without our help, Tavito?" I asked. "Yes . . . I can do it." replied Tavito . . . appearing to be steady on his feet. "Here I am little lamb." declared Tavito, "You were calling me . . . now come over and say hello!"

The lamb came right over to Tavito and put his front legs up on the corral fencing so that Tavito could stroke his snow white, wooly head. It was so beautiful! If I had not seen it with my own eyes, I probably would not have believed it. After petting the lamb for around 10 minutes we decided to return to the house. "Tavito," I began, "you did so well on the way over here . . . would you like to try to walk back to the house on your own? Antonio and I will stand right beside you, so if you need help we will be there for you."

"Yes, Br. Matthew," responded Tavito, "I can walk now

. . . I know I can; vamanos!" (Let's go!) And, yes . . . he did walk back to the house! Cuit yelled: "Wait, Tavito . . . we have to get your cot!" "I don't need it anymore Cuit," replied Tavito, "I'm going to sit on a chair!" Tavito was back! From that day on, Tavito continued to improve at record breaking speed; within 3 days he was back to normal.

Later that afternoon when I was resting in the mission hut, I couldn't help but reflect on the whole incident. Tavito had been brought almost to the point of death by an unfortunate accident with a venomous snake . . . and then was marvelously restored to health by a providential encounter with a gentle, little lamb. What kind of wondrous place was this? Even the humblest elements of the natural world seemed to be imbued with the capacity to heal!

Following another phenomenal period of reading and discussion, a strange thing happened that evening. The group had acquired at least 10 new participants, and the general comfort level of those present seemed to be on the rise. One individual named Tomas felt sufficiently at ease as to raise a question that had nothing to do with the reading but was, apparently, of great interest to many of the villagers.

"Br. Matthew," began Tomas, "have you heard the news regarding the kidnapping of the American businessman, Benjamin Lake?" "Yes, I am aware of the incident, Tomas." I responded calmly . . . but interiorly I was nervous, wondering where this question was going. "Well, he has been missing for weeks now . . . do you think he's OK?" "Yes, Tomas," I replied, "My guess is that he is probably doing fine." "Why do you say that, Brother?" asked Tomas. "Because, Tomas . . . God is good!" I declared. "Of course . . . you are right, Brother!" exclaimed Tomas. "Brother, Antonio told us you were from New York City and they say Mr. Lake is from New York City as well. By any chance, have you ever met him?"

"Yes, Tomas," I replied . . . cautiously; realizing that the day would come when the people in front of me would learn that "Br. Matthew" had in fact been Benjamin Lake. "I met him at a social event in NYC a few years ago." "What was he like?" asked Tomas. "I didn't have much time with him but he struck me as being a hard-charging, jet-setter type businessman. I met him again just recently, however, and he seemed different. I bumped into him in the chapel of San Nicolas on the day he disappeared. He was there all by himself immersed in prayer."

Antonio was staring at me, but he didn't look nervous. He seemed to realize that I was preparing the villagers for the day when they would know the truth. "You know, Brother," began Tomas, "San Nicolas is the chapel that we, the indigenous, were supposed to use; it was built for us. Do you think Mr. Lake could have been praying for us?" "It wouldn't surprise me at all, Tomas." I replied, "But he also may have been asking for the intercession of the countless holy indigenous who have worshipped there over the centuries."

"Br. Matthew," said Tomas, "I have an idea. Why don't we say a prayer for Mr. Lake? Perhaps he *was* asking for the intercessory help of our faithful ancestors; but we, the living indigenous, can also pray for him. He seems like a good man and, right now . . . considering the situation he is in, he could probably use our help. Brother, could you possibly lead us in a prayer for him?"

With such a manifestation of thoughtfulness and charity, I was tempted to come clean and tell them the truth about myself. But my survival depended on my new, secret identity . . . and I was intent on staying alive! "Of course, Tomas . . . what a wonderful idea!" I said, "How about this: I will open the prayer, and since we are here in Raul's home, he can finish the prayer. Then we can conclude our meeting with all of us praying together the Lord's Prayer." "Yes, Brother," replied Tomas, "that would be perfect."

"Lord," I began, "we turn to you this evening asking you to help Benjamin Lake. He is in a very unusual situation, Lord . . . help him to pray; help him to trust you and to depend on you. OK, Raul . . . your turn." "Good Lord Jesus," began Raul, "we ask you to watch over our brother, Benjamin Lake. He is a captive, Lord; set him free! In Luke 4: 18, you said: *I have been anointed to release the captives and to set free the oppressed.* My people know what it is like to be oppressed, Lord. We know what Mr. Lake is experiencing. Hear the prayers of a man who, on the day he was taken, was seen praying in the ancient, humble chapel of my people. Let him come away from this experience a better, holier person. I call on the intercession of holy Juan Diego and La Virgencita de Guadalupe. AMEN."

We finished up with the Lord's Prayer and as people began to disperse Tomas and Antonio approached me. "We just received word, Brother," began Antonio, "that a jaguar visited our village this evening . . . Tavito's father found fresh tracks behind his house. Sometimes, an older jaguar who can no longer hunt very well will try to find easy prey in a village. They will target the sick or the elderly who are bedridden and helpless. Then they wait until the vulnerable person is left alone with the door open. And when no one is around to see it, the jaguar will sneak into the house, kill the person, and drag the corpse back into the forest. So . . . just to be safe, Tomas and I will accompany you on your return to the mission house."

"Thank you . . . I appreciate it." I said, "Of course, after that little story, I probably won't be able to sleep tonight!" "You don't have to worry, Brother." explained Antonio, "As long as your door is closed and secured you have nothing to fear."

CHAPTER FIFTEEN

After a delicious, hot breakfast of freshly made corn tortillas, refried beans, bananas and coffee, I left Raul's home and returned to the mission house for a little reading and relaxation. There weren't many books in the hut, but there certainly were a sufficient number to keep me occupied for a few days. As Cicero, a great Roman politician and writer, said: *If you have a garden and a library, you have everything you need.* The 8 books at my disposal could have been considered a library only if one was willing to factor in the incredible remoteness of that particular location. But with regard to the garden; I was in the middle of the original, prototype of all gardens; the one designed by the Creator himself.

I decided to review the Directory that listed the plants and animals represented in the *Montes Azules Biosphere Reserve*. It was fascinating! The biodiversity of that ecosystem was just stunning! I was particularly impressed with the hundreds of species of trees native to the region. The book provided very well done, color drawings of some of the more prevalent tree species. After reading about 4 or 5 of the most common trees and studying the drawings, I decided to go for a little walk to see if I would be able to recognize them. I wanted to learn as much as I could about this wondrous place that was having such a beneficial and transformative effect on me. I also thought it would help me in my relationship with the villagers if I could converse intelligently with them about the rainforest.

I walked to the far end of the village and spotted a rather wide opening in the brush that appeared to be a trail for the carts used in association with the planted fields the people were developing. As I meandered along this unusually clear trail, I was looking around at the trees and checking the book to see if I could identify the species and distinguish one from another.

My first "botanical excursion" was going quite well; I quickly recognized 2 of the most numerous trees in the rainforest. At the same time, I detected some sort of slight movement in the trail around 75 feet in front of me but I didn't think much of it because there were birds, lizards, and who knows what else moving all around me. Suddenly, I sensed that movement again and this time I realized there was something unusual about that particular movement . . . it was totally silent.

Immediately, I stopped walking, strained my eyes and tried to make out what, if anything was moving in the trail ahead of me. What I saw caused me to stop breathing . . . and I'm lucky it didn't cause my heart to stop beating! There was a full grown jaguar crouched down very low to the ground along the side of the trail, and it was moving in my direction ever so slowly. It was obvious that he had been stalking me and was now preparing to attack. Thoughts began to race through my head; how foolish I was to wander into the forest knowing that a hungry jaguar was casing the village. Did the Lord bring me this far only to have me mauled and disemboweled by a jaguar? I recalled what I had just read in the Directory . . .

that due to the unusual strength of its bite, the jaguar had a unique way of instantly killing its prey; it drives its huge teeth directly into the victim's skull!

Without taking my eyes off the jaguar, and before I could take another breath . . . I sensed a presence behind me: "Don't move a muscle, Br. Matthew. It's me, Juan. I see the jaguar. Do exactly what I tell you. Stand perfectly still. I am going to slowly pass in front of you. Then I am going to run off to the right into that little clearing. The jaguar will chase me because his instinct is to go for prey that appears to be afraid. Don't worry about me . . . I know what I'm doing. Remember . . . DO NOT MOVE!"

I couldn't imagine what he was planning to do with the jaguar, but I certainly wasn't about to discuss the question. Forget about the jaguar's instinct! My instinct was demanding that I take flight . . . immediately! But I had seen enough of the Mayan people to know that they knew their world better than I knew my own. Although I only met Juan once and really didn't know him . . . I had to trust him. What would I do if the jaguar got hold of Juan? What would I do if the jaguar came straight at me? I recalled an article I once read about a villager in Africa who killed a leopard by plunging his fist and arm down the leopard's throat . . . choking it to death. I decided right then and there to do the same thing if I were attacked, only in my case, knowing that a jaguar is bigger than a leopard, I was planning to shove the Directory down his throat as well!

Juan was now directly in front of me and the jaguar was about 50 feet away. The jaguar came to a halt and gave a little snarl. I was so terrified I thought for sure I would pass out . . . but I didn't. In fact, because of the adrenalin rush, all my senses were keener and more alert than normal . . . so much so that it seemed like I could actually smell the animal. My vision became so acute that I thought I noticed something irregular about the shape of the creature. I couldn't figure out what it was but something seemed "off".

Suddenly, without any warning, Juan took off to the right like a racehorse out of the gate! And, like a greyhound chasing the rabbit, the Jaguar gave chase . . . just as Juan predicted. The jaguar, as if he was shot out of a cannon, tore after Juan. The big cat was only around 25 feet away from me and was closing quickly on Juan. Suddenly Juan, with the ferocious cat only 10 feet or so behind him, leapt into the air as though he was in a long jump competition. When Juan landed on the ground I looked to see where the jaguar was, expecting him to descend upon Juan and tear him to pieces, but the enraged creature was gone; he simply disappeared!

What kind of Mayan magic, or miracle, was this? I wasn't sure if it was OK to move now . . . but not knowing where the jaguar was I decided to stay put. Juan came running towards me yelling: "Let's go Brother, let's get out of here quickly! Come on . . . back to the village!" Juan grabbed me by the arm and we began to run. "What happened to the jaguar . . . where is he?" I asked . . . still trembling from shock and adrenalin but elated that Juan had not been hurt. "I led him directly into a pit cave!" declared Juan, "It's 20 feet deep, and I don't think he can get out, but you never know . . . jaguars are good climbers! We can recruit some men from the village and return to check on him."

When we returned with 2 men, both of them armed with heavy spears, we saw the jaguar at the bottom of the pit cave and he appeared to be dead. The men dropped a few golf ball size stones on him to see if he was alive and the animal had no reaction at all. One of the men had enough foresight to bring along some metal hooks and some rope so that, in the event the jaguar was dead, we would be able to hoist him out of the pit.

We quickly realized that it would be almost impossible for us to lift a 300-pound, dead jaguar out of a 20-foot hole in the ground, so Juan ran back to the village and returned with a horse. We set the hooks and fastened the ropes to the horse and the big cat was up and out of the pit cave in just a few seconds. As we examined the beautiful animal we discovered that it had an enormous, internal tumor that was causing the left side of its body to be grossly misshapen. This explained the bodily distortion I thought I noticed on the cat when I first saw him.

It also explained why the poor creature was casing the village looking for an easy meal. Juan explained that he decided to follow me at a distance when he saw me entering the forest and leafing through the Directory. He said that he spotted the jaguar long before I did and remembered that there was a pit cave about 15 yards from where I had been standing. "Juan," I said, "You risked your life to save mine? You didn't have to do it; you could have pretended you never saw the jaguar and allowed it to attack me. But you didn't. You were prepared to lay down your life for me! Why, Juan? Why were you willing to sacrifice yourself for me . . . a stranger; someone you just met a few days ago?"

"You are not a stranger," began Juan, "you are my brother! Also, you are our guest . . . we are responsible for your safety." On the evening that I did the reading about how St. Francis of Assisi converted the robbers, Juan was the individual who shared the beautiful insight regarding the "expansion of the good;" comparing the conversion of the robbers to the pacification of the wolf of Gubbio and pointing out how in both instances a single act of charity was marvelously fruitful . . . producing many "winners" at various levels!

"The way I see it, Juan," I said, "the heroic act of charity that you did today is comparable to what St. Francis did with the wolf of Gubbio. The wolf was not deranged and dying . . . but the jaguar was. So, by putting your life at risk and leading the desperately ill cat into the pit cave, you not only put him out of his misery, but you also saved me, as well as your entire village, from the death and destruction the unfortunate, diseased creature would have certainly brought about." "You see, Brother," responded Juan joyfully, "we can do good, but we cannot presume to completely control the good because it is always done in communion . . . for, as Jesus said: *Only God is good* (Mark 10: 18). The good we do radiates unto eternal life! With this in mind, Brother . . . what better way to thank and repay the person who healed my son, Tavito, than to save him from a marauding jaguar! The good *you* did made me feel closer to you . . . and that is why I was concerned and followed you into the forest." Up until that point, I didn't realize that Tavito was Juan's son.

CHAPTER SIXTEEN

The next few days were very peaceful and relaxed. I visited 2 families each morning and spent the rest of the day reading, praying, and reflecting. I devoured Augustine's *Confessions* and was beginning to go through the volume that recounted the life story of Bartolomé de Las Casas. I passed a couple of hours each day just sitting peacefully in the chapel and, little by little, I was beginning to find the heart I had lost. Sometimes . . . we have to stop everything in order to discover the truth about ourselves. I discovered that if I didn't run away from silence and inactivity, not only did I and the world not fall apart, but I felt much closer to God, myself, others . . . and creation.

At night, the orphic tranquility was so penetrating that the feelings associated with loss and grief, which I had so unwisely suppressed, surfaced and I would find myself weeping in the middle of the night. As difficult as this was, it was all part of the healing and renewal that was taking place in my life. Juan could sense that I was experiencing some difficult emotions. "Br. Matthew," began Juan, "you are carrying something heavy in your heart . . . I can feel the sadness in your spirit. I don't like the idea of your being alone at night in the mission house; so starting tonight I will be sleeping in the chapel. I will be there, right next door to you, if you need anything."

I thought to myself: "How did I go from not having a single friend I could trust . . . to having a number of friends who loved me so much they would lay down their life for me without hesitation?" And here was Juan . . . anticipating my needs and sacrificing his comfort zone so that I would be more comfortable. Without being fully aware of how it all happened, I was making beautiful friends; and these new friends were having an incalculable, positive impact on my life! I couldn't help but recall how Cicero, in the philosophical dialog, *Laelius De Amicitia* (Laelius on Friendship) . . . pointed out that friendship has a wonderful way of doubling our joy and dividing our grief.

At the same time, I couldn't help but wonder if in my study of the foundations of Western Civilization, I and so many others had been focusing too much on the cultural contributions received from Greece and Rome while not appreciating sufficiently the cultural traits of less studied civilizations . . . many of which could be helpful in terms of balancing or complementing our own imperfect, cultural milieu. For example: the happiness and contentment the Mayan people displayed while lacking the panoply of material possessions considered to be a basic requirement for happiness in western societies. What is it that shields them from falling prey to consumerism and its dehumanizing effect? Does it have something to do with the extraordinarily integrated relationship they have with God, his creation, and one another? Perhaps some degree of poverty . . . the renunciation of *having* more in favor of *being* more . . . is itself a type of inoculation that protects people from the ravages of materialism and radical individualism.

After all . . . there must be some reason why Jesus, the Savior of the world, chose to live in poverty. Did that choice contain a message for us? Didn't Jesus say that it would be easier for a camel to pass through the eye of a needle than for a rich man to enter the kingdom of God? (Matthew 19: 24) Perhaps, then, it is the Gospel itself that has been underappreciated and insufficiently understood in terms of its role as a necessary and primary contributor to the foundation of any fully human civilization.

Reflection and contemplation seemed to be as much a part of this place as the toucan and the jaguar. It was impossible not to be touched by the simplicity and beauty that were present everywhere one looked. The village, the people, the natural environment . . . all facilitated reflection the way the cloister in a monastery engenders contemplation. Fr. Bill had said that I would see and experience things in Santa Maria de Guadalupe that I had never seen or experienced before; he could not have been more accurate in his wise prognostication.

One morning after breakfast, Raul told me that we were in for a very pleasant surprise; Fr. Bill would be arriving late that afternoon. Present in his entourage would be Esperanza and her daughter Rosario. "This is wonderful news, Raul!" I exclaimed, "It has been only eight days since I last spoke with Fr. Bill; nevertheless . . . I've had so many new and amazing experiences here that it feels like 10 years have passed!" "Well, Br. Matthew, I'm sure the two of you will have many lively discussions. We will set up another bed in the mission house for Fr. Bill, and we will leave a guitar next to his bed. Fr. Bill loves to play when he is here!" explained Raul, "Esperanza and Rosario will be staying with Juan and his family." "Is Juan related to Esperanza and Rosario?" I asked. "Yes,

Brother," replied Raul, "Juan is Esperanza's son; he and Rosario are fraternal twins."

When I went to Raul's house that evening for dinner, Fr. Bill was already there . . . he had arrived 10 minutes before me. We greeted one another warmly and then proceeded to enjoy a wonderful dinner with Raul and his family. Fr. Bill explained to our hosts how exhausted he was from his journey, so, after he announced that he would celebrate mass the next day at 11am, we excused ourselves and the 2 of us retired to the mission house.

"You're looking great, Br. Matthew!" exclaimed Fr. Bill as he stretched his tired bones out on his canvas cot, "Antonio has already told me about your 'high-stakes' conversation with the thug in front of the trafficker's house and how you attempted to evangelize him. Just keep praying for him Brother. I've also heard that you've been having quite an adventure here." "Really . . . Fr. Bill?" I asked. "You'd be amazed, Brother, at how well the 'grapevine' works in this part of the world," explained Fr. Bill. "I heard all about your readings and the great discussions, the healing of little Tavito . . . and your encounter with the jaguar! But what I don't know is what does all of this mean to you? Has this been a good experience for you? Have you sensed the Lord speaking to your heart through the transparent goodness of the poor and the simplicity of our Father's creation?

My cot was about 5 feet away from, and parallel to, Fr. Bill's, and I positioned myself in such a way that when I was lying on my back with my head propped up on a big, straw-filled pillow I would be facing Fr. Bill. I could sense that this conversation was going to be special. I considered Fr. Bill to be the mentor of the "new and improved" version of Benjamin Lake. Just as my new hero, St.

Augustine, had St. Ambrose to guide him . . . I had Fr. Bill.

"Fr. Bill," I began, "the Spirit has done so much with me in the short period of time I have been here that I can barely recognize myself . . . or I should say; I have grown so much, I feel like a new creation!" "I'm so, so happy to hear that, Brother! Based on your openness I felt certain that God would bless you here. Have you been reading the *Confessions*?" "Non-stop, Fr. Bill." I responded, "I've already read through the whole volume."

"Did anything in particular jump out at you?" inquired Fr. Bill. "Yes Fr. Bill," I answered, "many things, but one short line from book IV has stayed with me: *For what am I to myself without you, but a guide to my own downfall*." "What a wonderful insight, Brother!" exclaimed Fr. Bill. "I can't say I remember that line, but it sounds like classic Augustine. I don't mean to interrupt you, Brother . . . please, continue."

"I've done a great deal of reflection, Fr. Bill, on how my shallow, worldly lifestyle was the fruit of the cold, heartless person I had become when I drifted away from God. I had become completely self-absorbed and indifferent to the sufferings and needs of others. That's why that line from Augustine caught my attention. I realized, existentially . . . that is, from my own lived experience, that without God the only direction a person can move in . . . is down."

"I drifted away from God, Fr. Bill, because I found a new god . . . money. I thought my new god was more reliable, more controllable, and more enjoyable. I traded in everything that is good and true, everything that is innocent and pure, everything that has lasting, authentic value . . . for dust; for an illusion! As Virgil said in book III of the Aeneid: *To what extremes won't you compel our hearts, you accursed lust for gold?* Did my new god bring me the happiness it promised? Not at all! I was feeling more dejected and lost with each passing day! Never have I felt such hopelessness and isolation as when I became a devotee of the god of money."

"If it were not for the grace of God, Brother," replied Fr. Bill, "you would still be adrift in a wasteland of hedonistic and materialistic pursuits. As the great Roman poet, Horace, so aptly pointed out: *The mind enamored with deceptive things, declines things better.* I, too, have spent some time among the ancients, Brother!" "It's a wonderful line, Fr. Bill. Do you recall where it is from?" I asked. "Of course, I do, Brother. It's from the *Satires,* Book II... *Adclinus falsis animus meliora recusat.*"

"Fr. Bill . . . this is incredible!" I exclaimed, "Why didn't you tell me you were a Latinist?" "I was intending to, Brother," answered Fr. Bill, "but something told me to wait . . . until today. You see, Brother Matthew, the Latin copy of Augustine's *Confessiones* you found in the chapel of San Nicolas was mine . . . I left it there by accident the day before. It was an extremely unusual thing for me to do . . . and up until this day, I still don't understand how I could have forgotten it; I treasured it so."

"Occasionally, it was my custom to get a little exercise by walking to the Cathedral Zócalo with some taquitos for the boys. I would then spend an hour or so in the chapel of San Nicolas praying and reading my Latin copy of the *Confessiones.* But I was always very careful not to leave the book behind . . . it would be very difficult to replace. That night when I was about to fall asleep, suddenly, to my horror, I realized that I had left 'Augustine' behind in the chapel. I begged the Lord to watch over it until I could retrieve it sometime the next day . . . and you, Brother, were the answer to that prayer! As you were telling me the amazing story of how you came across the book, I knew immediately that God was doing something marvelous . . . and that St. Augustine was in on it!"

"It is truly amazing for me to observe how God is working in your life, Brother." continued Fr. Bill. "He brought you here to the Mayan village of Santa Maria de Guadalupe in the *Montes Azules Biosphere Reserve* so you could hear for the first time . . . the cry of the poor, and the cry of the earth! He wanted you to know the truth from which you so effectively shielded yourself; that you and I, all of us, are responsible for the earth and for the poor. The poor are not a category or a statistic . . . they are our brothers and sisters, our family . . . our friends! And the earth is not something we can use and abuse in any way we choose. It is a precious gift from our Father that we must care for with great sensitivity and gratitude."

"Are you with me, Brother, or am I moving too fast?" "You're not going too fast, Fr. Bill . . . I'm getting it all; please, continue." "OK, Brother. The reality that has been overlooked and at times, flatly rejected, is that everything is interrelated; the human environment and the natural environment are connected . . . they rise or fall together. This is simply the way it is . . . it's an inescapable reality that we have in fact tried our best to ignore. And the damage that has come into the world as a result of this lapse in humility, this foolish attempt to evade the truth, is all around us."

"I know you are aware of the environmental movement, Brother, because I remember you mentioned that it was a factor that was bound to stand in the way of your desire to plunder the Biosphere Reserve for its oil deposits. But this movement, regardless of how well intentioned . . . is bound to fail; because it does not recognize that the environment cannot be isolated from its integral relationship with the poor . . . and with God!"

"Basically, Brother," continued Fr. Bill, "what I'm trying to say here is that what most people are calling an "ecological crisis' . . . or a 'socioeconomic crisis'; is actually a spiritual crisis! Are we really to believe that people will show a great and sustained concern for the vulnerable creatures of the natural environment when they manifest little or no interest at all in the most vulnerable members of their own species? And if man does not respect his own natural and moral structure, what are the chances he will display respect for the authentic nature of any other creature?"

"The root problem, Brother, is this; when people believe and live as though what *Nietzsche* said is true . . . I'm referring of course to his announcement that *'God is dead"* . . . then all that remains is man; an anemic, counterfeit version of man to be sure! But sadly, it is this truncated rendition of man that ends up being isolated and alienated . . . wandering about, lost and alone in the darkness. This misguided and ill-fated anthropocentrism is what's driving many of our contemporary problems, such as a wasteful and compulsive consumerism . . . in which we and our planet are the ones consumed; an obsessive desire for, and attachment to, material things; an endless, self-destructive search for more and greater pleasure . . . with the concomitant requirement of avoiding any and all pain, sacrifice, and discomfort; and, finally, an individualism that is so fanatical that the very concept of the 'common good' is perceived as an enemy of personal freedom and human rights."

"Are you still with me, Brother?" asked Fr. Bill, "I know

I've put a lot out there!" "I'm with you, Fr. Bill, I'm with you . . . don't stop; I need to hear this," I answered. "This mindset tends to foster a utilitarian outlook where beauty and goodness have no place; the only thing that matters is how useful or productive something, or someone, is. This utilitarian perspective is probably, in itself, the *least* productive attitude a society could adopt! It has given us what is commonly referred to as the 'throw-away' society.

"Wow, Fr. Bill . . . that can't be good; a 'throw-away' society?" I remarked, "So where do we go from here . . . is there a way forward?" "Yes, Brother . . . there is a way." replied Fr. Bill, "It's called . . . *The Civilization of Love.*" "OK, Fr. Bill . . . now, I am lost! I've never heard of such a thing as *The Civilization of Love.*" "It begins, Brother," explained Fr. Bill, "with an accurate and authentic anthropology . . . where man is understood correctly as having been created by a loving Father and, therefore, has immense dignity and is defined by his relationship with God, others, and creation. From this truth about man flows the truth concerning the family, which is always based upon marriage between a man and a woman. This, in a nutshell, is the foundation for *The Civilization of Love.*"

"I have to say, Fr. Bill," I began, "when you were describing the various components of our misguided, anthropocentric, 'throw-away' culture . . . I recognized myself in there; that was precisely the way I used to think." "I know, Brother," replied Fr. Bill, "that's why I shared with you such a detailed explanation; I wanted you to understand exactly what it was you fell into when you 'threw-away' your moral compass."

"So, Fr. Bill," I began, "I guess The Civilization of Love will require the introduction of many new laws." "I wish it were that simple, Brother." explained Fr. Bill, "When the corruption of a culture is such that it no longer accepts objective truth and fails to observe universally valid principles . . . laws are experienced as nothing more than obstacles that are arbitrarily imposed and therefore do not deserve respect. Consequently, political or legislative efforts to protect the poor and the environment . . . or anything else that is vulnerable, precious and in need of protection . . . will not suffice."

"The transformation, Brother, begins in the heart of man; as you yourself have just recently experienced. From this new heart will flow, not just proper laws, but more importantly . . . a culture and lifestyle that is worthy of man's high calling and dignity; a civilization of love! Remember, Brother, what Jesus, the Lord of Love taught us: . . . *where your treasure is, there will your heart be also . . .* Matthew 6:21."

"Brother . . . I'm going to play a song that is based on the spirituality of St. Francis. See if this doesn't speak to your own life experience." Fr. Bill reached for the guitar beside his bed and began playing and singing:

Brother Sun and Sister Moon, I seldom see you, seldom hear your tune;

preoccupied with selfish misery.

Brother Wind and Sister Air, open my eyes to visions pure and fair.

That I may see the glory around me!

I am God's creature, of him I am part.

I feel His love awakening my heart.

Brother Sun and Sister Moon, I now do see you, I can hear your tune.

So much in love with all that I survey!

"What a beautiful song, Father!" I said, "I recognize the tune . . . Donovan: *Brother Sun, Sister Moon* . . . but I never paid any attention to the words. Now, however, listening closely to the words . . . I feel like it was written for me!"

"Well, Brother Matthew, I think I've given you enough to reflect on for a few days. Allow me to shift the conversation to something I really need to discuss with you." "Of course, Fr. Bill," I replied, "what's up?" "Have you heard the news about what's happening in San Cristobal?" asked Fr. Bill. "No, Fr. Bill . . . I haven't heard anything at all about San Cristobal."

"The economy is falling apart!" explained Fr. Bill, "Since the kidnapping of Benjamin Lake, which supposedly was perpetrated by the indigenous, the tourists are afraid to visit San Cristobal. Many people are being laid off, and others are being let go altogether. It's causing a great deal of suffering; some families are on the verge of losing their homes. Most people assume that you have been murdered because it's been over a month since you went missing, and no one has seen or heard from you since."

"This is why the time has come for you to return to the USA. Once you are safe on US soil, you can tell the world the truth; that, far from kidnapping you, it was the indigenous that rescued and protected you. The real culprits who attempted to kidnap you were a greedy government official and an opportunistic drug cartel. The quicker the truth gets out, the better, Brother. The situation is very serious . . . even Esperanza and Rosario have been laid off and are down to their last few pesos." "Wow, Fr. Bill . . . what a disaster!" I exclaimed. "But there is hope, Brother," explained Fr. Bill. "I believe that when the world learns of how the poor indigenous people helped you; how the orphans secreted you away from the kidnappers . . . and how Juan saved you from the jaguar; the tourist business will explode in San Cristobal!"

"I couldn't agree with you more, Fr. Bill . . . on both counts; that there is hope, and that I have to get back to the States immediately. But how can I return to the USA without being intercepted by the police or some other government entity? Have you given that any thought?"

"I have, Brother, and what's more, I prayed over this question for days. Here's how it works, Brother. You don't have to get to the USA proper . . . in the sense of crossing the international border . . . you just have to make it to a US Embassy or Consulate. The Embassy in Mexico City is too far . . . 12 hours from San Cristobal. The Consulate in Merida is much closer, and I know an archeologist in Palenque who will take you there. Merida is around 7 hours by car from Palenque, and Palenque is 3 hours from here. Mario is staying in Santa Maria tonight and right after mass tomorrow, he will drive you to Palenque. I told Mario you wanted to tour the famous Palenque ruins. The following day my archeologist friend will take you to the Consulate in Merida. Once you are safe in the Consulate, you will be able to contact your pilot, and he can come and get you. What do you think, Brother, are you OK with this plan?"

"It's brilliant, Fr. Bill!" I exclaimed, "The idea of an Embassy or a Consulate never entered my mind; probably because I was so focused on getting back, physically, to the safety of my own country. It sounds like you may have already spoken with the archeologist in Palenque . . . and by the way; what is Palenque?" "Good question, Brother," answered Fr. Bill, "Palenque is a series of very important

Mayan ruins. It's very popular with the tourists and so a small town has developed there as well. My friend has the use of a relatively comfortable house, and you will be able to take a shower, eat a good dinner, and rest soundly in preparation for your trip."

"By any chance, did you share with him my real identity?" I asked. "No, Brother. He just knows that a Franciscan Friar named Br. Matthew needs a lift to the US Consulate in Merida. He was already planning to go to Merida to do a few chores, so it worked out well. He also said he was looking forward to meeting you and was glad he would have someone to converse with on such a long trip."

"What is this archeologist's name?" I asked. "His name is Dr. Ross." answered Fr. Bill. "Did he study archeology at Harvard?" I asked. "Yes . . . as a matter of fact, he did." responded Fr. Bill. "Is his first name Julian?" "YES! Do you know him?" "I do indeed, Fr. Bill," I replied, "We bumped into one another from time to time on campus. I used to go jogging with him, and we had a number of discussions about ancient Roman archeological discoveries. He's a great guy, but I didn't get to know him that well because he was finishing up his post-graduate studies, and I was just beginning mine. We were on campus together for just one academic year."

"This is fantastic, Brother!" exclaimed Fr. Bill, "Talk about divine providence!" "Do you think I should tell him who I really am?" I asked. "Yes, Brother," answered Fr. Bill, "I don't think there would be any harm in doing so. Just about everyone in Mexico, as well as in the USA, knows about Benjamin Lake; you've practically become a household name. Chances are . . . after an overnight in his residence and a 7-hour drive, he's going to recognize who you really are anyway. I think it would be best, therefore, to share with him the whole story. Be prepared, however, for the possibility that he might be a little nervous about traveling with you. Remember, Brother . . . *everyone* is looking for you. If you ever get pulled over by the police, they might arrest Dr. Ross."

"You're so right, Fr. Bill." I said, "But let me share this with you about Julian: he's the most courageous and adventurous person I have ever known; the only one who even comes close is Teddy Roosevelt! Julian's nickname on the Harvard campus was . . . *The Magnate for Adventure*. It didn't matter what you did with him (walking across the campus to the bookstore, for example), some unusual series of events would transpire, turning what would normally be a trance-inducing stroll into an unforgettable adventure comparable to the *Lewis and Clark Expedition!*"

"OK, Brother . . . sounds good! I guess that's why he became an archeologist!" exclaimed Fr. Bill. "No question about it, Fr. Bill . . . the 'Magnate' is in his element among those ancient ruins and the impenetrable rainforest." "Good . . . then, he will probably enjoy the whole experience of taking you to Merida." said Fr. Bill, "Well . . . that just about covers it, Brother. Do you have any questions?" "Yes, Father, one question: you said that Esperanza and Rosario are here. I'm wondering what kind of a reception I can expect from them tomorrow at mass; the last time I saw Esperanza she wanted to return me to the kidnappers!"

"Oh! Forget about that, Brother!" exclaimed Fr. Bill, "That's ancient history! They love you now, Brother! Rosario wears the crucifix you gave her all the time! Remember, Brother . . . Tavito is Esperanza's grandson; if she and Rosario could have their way . . . you would be canonized at tomorrow's mass!" "I'm happy to hear that, Fr. Bill. They had every right to hold me in disdain because of the way I was; what a relief to know they are aware of how much I have changed."

CHAPTER SEVENTEEN

"We are here, Br. Matthew... this is Palenque." announced Mario. It was around 5:30 pm, and we had been traveling for a total of 5 hours . . . 2 hours on foot and 3 hours by car. "Hello there, Br. Matthew . . . welcome to my humble residence!" said Dr. Ross as I approached the front door of his house. The house was a simple design and constructed from tropical woods such as cedar and mahogany. There was a horse tied to a small tree in the front yard, and off to the right side of the house was a chicken coop. A dirt path led to the front porch, and on one of the posts was a sign which read: *Dr. Julian Ross, Archeology, Harvard University.*

"Thank you, Dr. Ross," I replied, "I appreciate your kind hospitality!" Dr. Ross was dressed in blue jeans, black flip-flops, and a loose fitting, tan polo shirt. He was about 6 feet tall with a very athletic build and medium length, chestnut colored hair. "Come in, Brother . . . you've had a long journey from the Reserve; you can relax now. You are not only my guest . . . you are the guest of Harvard University as well!

Standing beside Dr. Ross was a 3-foot tall, brownish colored monkey. "This is Pakal, Brother . . . he's my assistant; hey, if Dr. *'Indiana'* Jones can have *Sallah* . . . I can have Pakal! Pakal was the name of the most famous Mayan ruler to reign here in Palenque. We found this beautiful *Spider Monkey* after he had been attacked by a *Harpy Eagle*. Apparently, the eagle was tearing the monkey to ribbons with its powerful beak and razor sharp talons when, by some incredible stroke of luck, the terrified monkey managed to get its prehensile tail wrapped around the eagle's throat and succeeded in choking the apex predator to death."

"Wow!" I exclaimed, "He must be an exceptionally intelligent monkey!" "Oh . . . he's a brilliant creature, Brother! Here, watch this: Pakal . . . take Br. Matthew's bag to his room please." Immediately, Pakal picked up my bag, went into the house and placed the bag on the bed in the guest room. "Pretty impressive, wouldn't you say, Brother?" declared a very proud Dr. Ross. "Amazing!" I replied.

We went into the spacious living section of the house, which was a combination kitchen, dining room, and sitting area. I collapsed into a very comfortable sofa, and who came out of nowhere to sit right next to me? Pakal! "He likes you, Brother! He doesn't do that with everyone." explained Dr. Ross. "I'm happy to know I've made a new friend! What does he do if he *doesn't* like someone?" I asked. "Are you ready for this, Brother?" said Dr. Ross, "He takes a strategic position above the person in question . . . then proceeds to piss all over the individual!" "Wow! Then what happens?" I asked. "The person screams . . . and Pakal laughs!" replied Dr. Ross, "Don't worry, Brother . . . in the past few years I have had countless people in this house and Pakal has gotten pissed off only twice! And in each incident, the dousing was more than merited!"

"Hey . . . is that a wild Parrot I see over there, Dr.

Ross?" I asked. "Yes, it is, Brother; she's a Scarlet Macaw, another rescue animal. She can fly, but only for very short distances. She has become a valued member of our household. Her name is *Lakamha* . . . which was the ancient name for Palenque. She knows how to talk, Brother. Walk over to her and say 'hello'. She likes the attention and will probably say something."

I rose from the couch and Pakal took my hand . . . so we walked together over to the Macaw. "Hello," I said, addressing the parrot and feeling at that moment very much like *Mowgli,* the main character in Rudyard Kipling's *The Jungle Book.* After a pause of about 10 seconds, Lakamha began to speak: "Benjamin Lake lives! Benjamin Lake lives! Viva! Viva! Benjamin Lake lives!"

"What's going on here?" I thought, "Does this Scarlet Macaw actually know who I really am? But how could that be?" I just stood there looking at her, frozen with confusion . . . then I turned and looked at Dr. Ross. "Let me explain, Br. Matthew," began Dr. Ross. "Benjamin Lake was a friend of mine at Harvard. I say friend . . . I'm not sure if he would describe me as *his* friend; he was from a powerfully wealthy family . . . so perhaps he would see me more as an acquaintance. But I saw him as a friend, and I really enjoyed our discussions. When I heard about his disappearance and how everyone was saying he was probably dead . . . I refused to believe it. And so, to buoy up my hope, I taught Lakamha to say . . . *Benjamin Lake lives!"*

"Every day, Br. Matthew," continued Dr. Ross, "I say a prayer for Benjamin. I ask the Lord to help him, and I tell the Lord to use me to find him. You know, Brother, no one is as familiar with this jungle as I am, and I have been on the alert and keeping an eye out for Benjamin in all my excursions into the rainforest. I told the Lord that I would sacrifice whatever archeological discoveries remain in my career if he would just allow me to find my friend Benjamin . . . alive."

"What would you do if you did find him?" I asked. "Oh, well . . . that's actually a good question, Brother; I never really thought about it. I guess I would just bring him down to the police station." "But isn't it possible the police were involved in his kidnapping? You don't really believe it was the indigenous, do you?" "No . . . not for a minute! I always suspected a drug cartel. But you're right about the police; that would be very risky." "So, then . . . if God decided to answer your prayer, what would you do with Benjamin?"

"I would take him to the American Consulate in Merida!" exclaimed Dr. Ross. "Perfect! Because that's where you *will* be taking him!" I replied, as I removed my straw hat and sunglasses, "Julian . . . your prayers have been answered. I'm your friend, Benjamin Lake!" "Wait," said a thoroughly confused Dr. Ross, "you're . . . you're *not* . . . Br. Matthew?" "No!" I exclaimed, "That's just my disguise. Here, watch, *Magnate for Adventure* . . . I'll take away my beard." I covered my entire beard with my two hands. "Yes! Yes! I can see you now . . . It's really you, Benjamin! This is amazing! I can't believe it! Thank you, Lord . . . Thank you! My friend was lost, but now . . . he is found!

I thanked Julian for being such a loyal friend . . . even though I had completely forgotten about him. We went on to discuss my situation for the rest of the evening with my giving due emphasis to how important it was that we avoid any contact with the police during our journey to Merida. Julian agreed 100% and assured me that he would drive directly to Merida without any intervening "adventures" of the sort for which *The Magnate* was famous. I told him in jest that I wasn't really sure he had any control over that aspect of his life, but I appreciated the sincerity of his good intention.

The house sitter, an older Mayan woman, showed up at 9am . . . at which point, Julian and I said goodbye to Pakal and Lakamha, put a few provisions in the back of Julian's white, 1995, Land Rover Defender and headed out for the 7-hour trip. Merida is on the northwestern tip of the Yucatan Peninsula. The *"White City,"* as it is sometimes called due to the unusually large number of white buildings . . . is an outgrowth of the ancient *Mayan City of T'ho*. For this reason, some historians consider Merida to be the oldest continually occupied city in the Americas.

As we journeyed, I shared with Julian how the Lord, by way of the attempted kidnapping, had taken me aside and transformed my heart. I explained how I had fallen into a moral decline that was so rapid and extreme that had it not been interrupted by the mercy of God, I would have surely ended in such condition as to give the Roman Emperor, Caligula, stiff competition for the title of . . . *Most Depraved!*

"I don't understand, Benjamin?" replied Julian, "When we were at Harvard you seemed like an awfully nice fellow." "Perhaps, in some respects, I was, Julian." I began, "But I was already beginning my descent into superficiality and worldliness. Slowly but surely . . . money, fame, power, and pleasure became more important to me than my relationship with God, his creation, others, and myself. I was being 'hollowed out' by these idols, and my interior life was decimated!"

"But from what I was hearing, Benjamin," said Julian,

"you went on to become super successful . . . a multi-billionaire!" "Yes, Julian; I am, by most accounts, one of the wealthiest people in the world. At the same time, however, I was a complete and total personal failure; one of the loneliest, most miserable individuals you could ever imagine! I gave myself over to worldly desire in the same reckless way that people of my genre have turned the entire global economy over to the invisible forces of the market and, heartlessly, interpret their undesirable effects on the poor and the environment as unavoidable, collateral damage!"

"So Benjamin," asked Julian, "Now that your heart has been healed and your spirit renewed, where will you go from here? What will you do when you return to New York tomorrow?" "That's the big question, Julian! I don't really know, yet; but, I know I'm not the same person, and therefore . . . I cannot live the same way I had been living; many things will have to change. I am no longer motivated by money, Julian. The only thing that moves me now is God's love. I want to serve him. Gone are the worldly idols of my past . . . and the personal slavery they demanded. Now . . . I am truly free; I live from the heart!"

"I envy you, Benjamin!" replied Julian, "And to think how they used to call *me*, "The Magnate for Adventure;" you're the one who is experiencing the most authentic of all adventures . . . the spiritual adventure! Benjamin . . . whatever direction you go in when you return to your life in the States, please stay in touch; I think we owe it to ourselves to maintain this unique, providential friendship with which we've been blessed."

"Absolutely, Julian." I said, "We're not just friends, Julian . . . we're brothers now!" "Brothers . . . that works for me, Benjamin!" replied Julian. "By the way, Julian," I said, "just to be safe . . . I think it would be best if you continue to call me Br. Matthew until we are safe in the Consulate. We might get into a conversation with someone on this trip and you could slip and call me Benjamin." "You're right, Benjamin . . . I mean, Br. Matthew!" replied Julian, earnestly.

CHAPTER EIGHTEEN

We were around 5 miles outside of Merida when the traffic began to slow down and back up. Finally, the cars came to a halt and we could see what was going on . . . a police check point. "I thought you said there were no check points on this route, Julian?" I asked in a state of nervous confusion. "Normally, there aren't, Brother. This is extremely unusual." replied Julian in an anxious tone.

"This is very dangerous, Julian." I said, "Will they ask for ID . . . because I don't have anything that proves I'm Br. Matthew." "No . . . Brother, they don't generally ask to see an ID at a police check point. Usually, they just ask where you are coming from, where you are going, and why. With the Harvard emblem on the side of our vehicle, I'm quite sure we won't have any problem." "I don't feel good about this, Julian. Do you think we could turn around and get into Merida by way of some back roads you might know about?" I asked. "I'm afraid we are now committed, Brother; turning back is not an option. Any vehicle that leaves the line would immediately be suspect and chased down. Once they were in the hands of the authorities, all the occupants of the vehicle would be subject to a thorough interrogation."

"Julian," I began, "you realize that, if they ever discover

who I am, you will probably be arrested for kidnapping. So . . . if they bring me inside for questioning, I think you should take off for the Consulate as fast as you can." "I would never make it, Brother. They would give chase and radio other units. The best thing, Brother is that we stay together . . . there is strength in numbers!" "That's a better idea, Julian . . . we'll work as a team. The thing that concerns me is that if they find out who I am, they may turn me over to the cartel . . . and they might want to silence you."

"Benjamin, I mean, Br. Matthew . . . listen to me," said Julian, "nothing is going to happen. Don't get yourself worked up. Relax . . . everything is going to be fine. I may even know some of the officers. I'm sure they will recognize my vehicle. Archeology and the tourism it produces is an enormous part of the economy here in the Yucatan." "OK . . . you're making a lot of sense, Julian. I'd better just calm down and take one thing at a time." I said. "Definitely, Brother." responded Julian, "We must be clearheaded and have our wits about us."

We were just one car away from the check point when I remembered something: "Julian! I just remembered something; do NOT tell the police we are headed for the US Consulate! We will say we're going to Merida to visit a couple of churches and to shop, OK? That's the purpose of our visit." "Got it, Brother . . . shopping and churches. Great; glad we got that straight . . . 30 seconds before our interview!"

"Hey, Brother," announced Julian with emotion, "we're in luck! I know this officer . . . his name is Nacho." "Fantastic, Julian!" I replied. "Hello, Dr. Ross. How are you today?" said the officer. "Great, Nacho! How about yourself?" answered Julian. "Oh . . . I've seen better days,

Dr. Ross." "What's the matter, Nacho . . . what's going on?" inquired Julian. "We were told to set up this check point just for today," began Nacho, "Supposedly our police chief received some kind of intel last night saying that Benjamin Lake and his kidnappers would be coming to Merida today. We were told that if we intercept him at this check point we should immediately turn him over to the 2 *Federales* who are across the street in that roadside diner. That's their car, right there in front . . . the black Mercedes."

"Ok, Nacho . . . all of that kind of makes sense to me; so what's the problem?" "The problem is . . . those 2 guys are *not* Federal Agents. They don't have badges or any other form of ID, and Federales don't drive around in luxury vehicles . . . nor do they have long hair, like one of them has. It's pretty obvious that they're cartel people." "I get it, Nacho. This really puts you on the spot, doesn't it?" "Yes, it does. Excuse me, Dr. Ross, but I see your passenger is a Franciscan. Do you mind if I ask him a question?" "Not at all, Nacho . . . his name is Br. Matthew," replied Julian.

"Brother Matthew," asked Nacho, "if I do come across Benjamin Lake today, is it wrong to turn him over to those 'Federales', as I was ordered to do?" "Yes, Nacho, it would be *very* wrong . . . for this reason; they are *not* Federal Agents, and you know it! You were told to turn Benjamin Lake over to the Federales. Well those guys have not proven to you that they are Federales, so to give Benjamin Lake to them would be contrary to your orders!"

"That's what I thought, Br. Matthew," replied Nacho, "thanks for confirming what my conscience has been telling me. So what *should* I do if I encounter Benjamin Lake today?" "Nacho . . . listen to me," I said. "You will not see Benjamin Lake today. Think about it . . . do you actually imagine he would come through here without wearing some sort of a disguise? He has probably already been through here and you didn't even recognize him!" "But what if I did recognize him . . . then what?" asked Nacho. "Under these circumstances, Nacho," I answered, "you do nothing . . . nothing at all. You just let him pass and be on his way."

"Thank you, Br. Matthew . . . I feel so much better now. I was so upset wondering what I should do if I ran into Benjamin Lake today. But thanks be to God I ran into you!" "Relax, Nacho." I said, "God sees the goodness in your heart, and he's watching over you. Be at peace my brother!" "Good to see you, Dr. Ross and Br. Matthew," said Nacho, as he extended his hand towards the road in front of us giving us permission to pass, "Have a great visit to Merida!"

"What did I tell you, Brother!" exclaimed Julian, "No problem . . . right through!" "OK, Julian . . . you called it. Nice going!" I replied. "Wow, Brother, the way you handled Nacho's 'Benjamin Lake' question . . . that was ingenious! I was sitting here in between the two of you sweating bullets! Boy . . . you played that one really close, Brother!" "Don't think that I wasn't nervous, Julian, because I most certainly was! Learning that the people who tried to kidnap me were just across the street was a real wake-up call for sure!"

"Brother," began Julian, "what was that check point all about? Do you think your kidnappers knew we were coming to Merida?" "I don't think so Julian. I think they are just fishing around out of desperation, you know . . . pulling out all the stops, as they say. At this point, they are probably just looking for someone . . . anyone . . . who knows anything about my whereabouts. So, I think that checkpoint has more to do with your special gift of being a magnate for adventure than with anything else; hey . . . I'm just kidding, Julian! But the incident does leave me with one concern; do you think the cartel might have scouts watching the Consulate? It might be dangerous for us to pull up there."

"No, Brother, not at all." replied Julian, "Don't worry about that . . . our troubles are behind us now; at this point, Brother, you're basically 'home free'! You see, Brother, the Consulate people are very experienced and sophisticated; there are usually at least 2 heavily armed guards posted at the entrance to the compound. The guards know that very often someone will try to stop an American citizen from reaching the Consulate . . . so if the bad guys are anywhere near the Consulate, *they* need to be worried! When we pull into the driveway, the guards will surround my vehicle and you will simply say . . . my name is Benjamin Lake; I'm a citizen of the United States of America."

CHAPTER NINETEEN

To say it felt weird to be back in Manhattan, NYC, would be something of an understatement. After everything I'd been through . . . the Franciscan orphanage, the Mayan village, the rainforest, etc., . . . not to mention the spiritual transformation I was experiencing, I felt like I was visiting the Big Apple for the very first time. That's not to say that I was having a positive experience of the city . . . because I wasn't. Having been immersed in the tranquil, fragile beauty of creation, I was appalled at the apparent chaos and congestion of the traffic . . . as well as the mindless pandemonium of the countless people who seemed to be rushing about aimlessly. I felt as though I was being swallowed whole by some sort of concrete and steel monster that feeds on a steady diet of programmed, semi-conscious human beings . . . preferably wearing business attire! "This can't possibly be the way human beings were meant to live!" I thought to myself.

Pancho picked me up in Merida and flew me into JFK; then a limo took me directly to my 5th Avenue apartment. I slept for 12 hours straight and woke the following morning with a ferocious appetite. After a breakfast more suitable for a lumberjack than a bank executive, I decided to walk to my office, 3 blocks away on Park Avenue. I dressed casual so as not to be recognized, but I did wear my colorful crucifix . . . which garnered some unwanted stares and a few raised eyebrows.

I made arrangements in advance to enter the building through the back, service entrance so as to avoid the Press and the bank employees. The first thing I had to do before I could tell my story to anyone was to speak with the Mexican government privately about the attempted kidnapping. After much reflection, I came to the conclusion that there was only one person I could safely share my story with . . . the President of Mexico, Miguel Uribe. I had already called Memphis and asked her to contact the President's office requesting an urgent, private teleconference at 12 noon.

The bank, together with my relatives, had organized an enormous dinner party for me that evening at *The Tavern On The Green* . . . a NYC icon in Central Park. Among the invited guests would be the mayor, the Mexican Consul General, a number of celebrities, many of the highest ranking business leaders of the city, and of course . . . reporters from all the major news outlets. Surely, the questions would be endless, so I wanted to be sure the President of Mexico heard everything first. But even if I was not able to connect with Miguel Uribe, in order to rescue the economy of San Cristobal, I would still have to make it clear that it was not the indigenous who attempted to kidnap me.

"I was able to reach *Los Pinos* (the 'White House' of Mexico)!" reported Memphis as I walked into my office, "The person I spoke with said the President is very anxious to speak with you and will call at noon for a private teleconference. That's five minutes from now, so let's make sure we are ready on our end." "Thank you,

Memphis; I'm glad he was available." I replied.

"Mr. Lake... I'm so glad to see you!" exclaimed the President, "Did the indigenous hurt you in any way?" "Mr. President, please . . . you may call me Benjamin." I replied. "This is a private conference, Benjamin, so feel free to call me Miguel." "The main thing I want to share with you, Miguel, is that the indigenous did not kidnap me. In fact, nobody kidnapped me! Someone attempted to kidnap me right in front of the Cathedral, but by the grace of God I escaped. The people who attempted to kidnap me, and who I have been hiding from for all this time, are members of a drug cartel called... *La Oscuridad.*

"It was the indigenous who saved my life! They hid me and protected me from the kidnappers until things calmed down and I was able to make it to Merida." "This is just incredible, Benjamin! So what was the purpose of that misleading ransom note?" asked the Mexican President. "Well, Miguel, this is where it gets a bit ugly; brace yourself for some upsetting news. The purpose of the note and the essential reason for the kidnapping was to destroy the reputation of the indigenous, which in turn would destroy all hopes of developing ecotourism in the area. Having undermined the credibility of the indigenous, it would then not only be possible to ignore them and drill for oil in the *Montes Azules Biosphere Reserve,* but drilling would then be the only viable option left for developing the region."

"But what does a drug cartel have to do with oil?" asked Miguel. "Nothing!" I answered, "I told you this was going to get ugly; the person who was actually behind all of this was your Secretary of Energy, Ricardo Villanueva!" "NO! It can't be, Benjamin . . . not Ricardo!" "I'm afraid so, Mr. President." I went on to explain everything in detail to the

Mexican President, and he was truly horrified at the greed and duplicity of one of the most trusted members of his administration. He was visibly shaken by the damage this one, heartless individual did to the good name of the beautiful indigenous people of his nation. He was also saddened to think of how a people who were already suffering economically were now faced with even greater economic woes due to this outrageous slander.

"Benjamin . . . listen to me." began the President, "People must know that the indigenous are innocent; I want the world to realize how noble they were in rescuing you! This, Benjamin, is what I am going to do and I must do it right away . . . because when the criminals hear that you are back in the USA and are telling your story they might abandon that house altogether and elude capture.

Therefore, I am going to send a special commando unit to raid that house immediately! Then, when we have them in custody, I'm sure they will give up Ricardo. I don't want the orphanage or anyone else in that neighborhood to be exposed to those dangerous people any longer. Once the criminals are removed from that house we can breathe easy. I'm sorry Benjamin, but I have to go now. Thank you so much for contacting me and sharing that sensitive information. I will call you soon to let you know how things are going. Adios!"

Following my conversation with President Miguel Uribe, I met with my cousin, Geoffrey, who, as vice president of *Praetergressus Bank,* had been running the bank in my absence. I told him that after the "welcome home" dinner that evening I would be heading out to my summer home in the Hamptons to recuperate for a couple of weeks. Therefore, he should continue to act as chief administrator of the bank. I couldn't tell if Geoff was pleased to see me, or if he was pleased that he would continue to be in charge of the bank. In any case . . . he appeared to be quite happy.

Following the dinner, my chauffeur drove me directly out to my home in the Hamptons, and we arrived a little after midnight. The 6-bedroom house sat on 2 acres of beautiful, beachfront property. Although it was an old house and practically a historical landmark, it had been recently refurbished and redesigned with "relaxation" being the guiding theme. Therefore, everything about the house was simple and laidback . . . right down to its natural cedar shakes. There was nothing ostentatious or luxurious about it; it was, as the Amish say . . . quite "plain". The house was surrounded by various gardens filled with sunflowers, geraniums, Montauk daisies, tulips, impatiens, and roses. Scattered across the property were strawberry plants and apple trees.

Just about everything in the house was made of wood, the floors, the furniture, the stairs, etc. As soon as you entered the house, you felt summoned to relax. There were 2 bedrooms downstairs and 4 upstairs. While the bedrooms were not particularly spacious, they all had splendid ocean views. The general aura of the house was similar to what one would expect in an out of the way refuge like *Gandhi's Ashram* in Sabarmati, India; an uncomplicated, low-tech environment, immersed in nature and natural materials such as leather, wool, cotton, wood, canvas, wicker, slate, and fieldstone.

I can't take any credit for the wonderful design; it was my Father's sister, my aunt Clare . . . who also happens to be my cousin Geoffrey's mother . . . who deserved recognition. Knowing how stressful my Father's life was, and realizing she would be breaking with convention, she came up with the idea of what she always referred to as "monastic simplicity". It's not easy to follow through so perfectly and consistently with a "less is more" design theme, while at the same time keeping it all balanced, human and realistic . . . but Clare did it. Anyone who ever stayed there said they dreaded the day they would have to leave and return to "the rat race". Because Clare said she experienced great serenity as she designed the house, Father, who was the original Latin enthusiast in our family, named the little estate, *Serenitatem*; which is Latin for . . . Serenity.

Despite all the accolades, I can't really say I liked the house. I stayed overnight there just once when the refurbishment was completed; and I did that just to please my aunt Clare. Put simply . . . the house was just not my speed. In my heyday, I was never in the mood for a quiet, retreat-like atmosphere; I wanted the nightlife, the noise, the comfort and the pleasure! As far as I was concerned the house wasn't similar to *Gandhi's Ashram* . . . it was more like St. Benedict's cave! And I wanted no part of it! Of course, I didn't have a fraction of the stress my father had; I didn't have a spouse, a child, or a major financial institution to watch over.

But now, after my spiritual experience with God's poor and his creation; after my encounter with Augustine, De Las Casas and Francis of Assisi; after absorbing the teachings of Fr. Bill and awakening to the truth about myself . . . *Serenitatem* was exactly where I needed to be! I had some serious discernment to do and that would require a good bit of prayer. The house had a small room that served as an office, complete with a laptop computer. Connected to the office was a small library room, which in turn was connected to a small sitting room. I decided to turn that sitting room into a temporary chapel.

I constructed a cross out of driftwood, tying two pieces together with a few long blades of dune grass. After hanging the cross on a wall, I moved the chairs back and placed pillows on the floor so I could sit or kneel while at prayer. Then I placed a hefty, white candle on a small, wooden table just below the driftwood cross and, *presto change-o*; sitting room becomes . . . the chapel of San Damiano!

The house boasted a very sizable wooden deck that faced the ocean, and I spent many hours there each day in reflection. If I wasn't in the chapel or on the deck, I'd be walking up and down the beach, asking the Lord to guide my steps into the future as smoothly as he guided the graceful seagulls that floated upon the ocean breezes and danced amidst the breaking waves. I could sense that the Lord was forming me to serve him in some way, but 4 days into my stay at Serenitatem . . . I still did not have perfect clarity with regard to my mission.

Then on the evening of day 5, at around 9pm . . . my calling started to clarify. I was sitting in the chapel reading Scripture when I stumbled upon Matthew 16: 24-26. One section impressed me in a most peculiar way . . . Jesus' words in line 25: *He who saves his life will lose it; but whoever loses his life for my sake will find it.* It suddenly struck me that the center of my life was the bank. And what are banks all about? Saving and storing up money, power and wealth! What I was sensing for the first time was that my heart had taken on the basic characteristics of a bank. I was applying to my personal life the same principles that are essential to banking; I was *saving* my life . . . not *giving* it away!

But Jesus already taught us about this phenomenon in

Matthew 6:21 . . . *Where your treasure is, there will your heart be also.* I knew right then and there I would have to give up the bank. This inspiration was as strong and clear to me as if the Lord had literally said to me: *"Hey, Benjamin . . . lose the bank!"* I resolved immediately to give the bank to my cousin, Geoffrey . . . and I had no doubt he would be more than happy to accept it.

By divesting myself of the bank, I would be free to serve the Lord in whatever way he indicated. But where was he leading me? What exactly did he want me to do once I was freed from my responsibilities at the bank? I concluded that he would most likely show me when I was fully formed and ready to receive the work. Maybe I needed additional formation. Should I go ahead and give Geoff the bank without even knowing what my future was going to be? Perhaps that was precisely what the Lord wanted from me . . . a radical act of faith. I decided to cross one bridge at a time and make the decision regarding the bank in the morning.

All the second floor bedrooms had enormous picture windows that extended 3 feet from the floor on up to 6 inches below the ceiling. The windows were 6 feet wide, with 2 sliding panes . . . each pane being 3 feet in width. The large glass panels slid on a track and disappeared into the wall. The windows did not have screens because they would have interfered with the spectacular view. Since it was late August, the air was generally hot and humid . . . not good weather for sleeping with the ocean view window open. But that particular evening a front came through from the North and the weather was Autumn-like and especially beautiful. So before going to bed, I opened the window completely . . . allowing the fresh ocean breeze to billow in and roll directly over my bed which was facing the window.

I can't imagine a more effective sleep remedy than the tranquil, somnolent sound of small waves gently splashing onto the sand, one after another; a peaceful symphony of dulcet, natural tones and harmonies . . . accompanied by the most aromatic, ocean fragrances imaginable. From my vantage point, lying on my back and staring out through a huge opening in the wall, I felt as if I was on a cloud that was floating over the coast. I could see everything; the beach, the breaking waves, the open sea, the horizon, the night sky illuminated by a waning crescent moon . . . and a plethora of stars.

Being submerged, as it were, in such breathtaking beauty, I couldn't help but reflect on how just a little more than a month ago I would not have even recognized, let alone valued, this wondrous manifestation of our Father's creation. I was very relaxed and a remarkable story Fr. Bill told me when I was at the orphanage surfaced and entered my consciousness. It was near Christmas and Father was visiting a Mayan village. He was talking with a group of children and, for some unknown reason, he asked a question for which he had no answer: *Why do you think God the Father wanted his son to be born in such a way that he would be completely surrounded by natural things like sheep, cows, donkeys, hay, wood, and stones?* An 8-year-old girl raised her hand and said: *Father... I know why he did that! Before my little brother was born, my mother spent many months knitting a beautiful blanket to cover her newborn baby. She wanted her innocent child to be surrounded by something beautiful that she herself had created . . . something that would communicate the love she had in her heart. That's what our Father did with his son; he surrounded him with the beauty and love of his own creation!*

Meditating on that wondrous insight and the transcendent peace of the nativity, I felt as if I was being reborn in the presence of the impoverished, holy family and God's humble creatures. Given such tranquil musings, it wasn't long before the lavish panorama of natural beauty set before me closed my eyes and drew me into the deepest recesses of that hidden, mysterious realm we call . . . sleep. As I was falling into that secret abode, I experienced a powerful sense of direction; somehow, I knew what my mission was. That's not to say I didn't already have an intuition regarding my future; I did. But I needed quiet time to see clearly what the Lord had done with me; he had given me a new life, a new love . . . a new heart! Consequently . . . my sleep that night was so restful, I felt as though I had been assumed into heaven!

CHAPTER TWENTY

Rising the following morning, I felt revitalized and invigorated with new purpose. This was not just the beginning of a new day for me . . . this was the beginning of a whole new life! After praying in the chapel, I enjoyed a light breakfast of cornflakes, milk, and bananas, then worked my way down to the beach for a morning stroll. As I walked barefoot in the sand, the water occasionally surging up and wetting my feet, I began planning the various things I wanted to do. First, I would have to meet with Geoffrey and discuss the transfer of the bank. Then, I would have to make plans for a new life in San Cristobal, Mexico. But before I could set up my mission of service to the indigenous in Chiapas, I wanted to discuss my ideas with the President of Mexico, Miguel Uribe.

When I arrived back at Serenitatem, exhilarated by the brisk walk and fresh, salt air, I got right down to business. "Good morning, Memphis," I said, "how are things going over there?" "All is well, Mr. Lake." responded Memphis, "You have one message: President Miguel Uribe called. He would like you to call him back . . . this morning, if possible." "Excellent! I was planning to call him this morning anyway." I replied, "Memphis . . . could you please tell Geoff I would like to meet with him at 1pm this afternoon at *The Plaza Hotel* on Fifth Avenue for *Afternoon Tea* at *The Palm Court*. Please call me back right away to confirm. And . . . oh, I almost forgot; don't worry about the limo. I'll use my Corvette . . . it's in the garage. Thanks, Memphis. Ciao!"

Five minutes later, my phone rang. It was Memphis: "Mr. Lake . . . Geoff wants to know if he can bring his mother, Clare. She loves *The Afternoon Tea* at *The Palm Court,* and he knows she would really enjoy joining the two of you." "Absolutely, Memphis; thanks . . . ciao!" Having squared away that important meeting, it was now time to touch base with Miguel Uribe.

"Hello, Mr. President, its Benjamin Lake." I said. "Now, remember, Benjamin . . . I am Miguel!" replied the president. "That's going to take a little getting used to . . . Miguel!" I countered. "Benjamin . . . I have some good news for you." began Miguel, "We raided the house and captured the traffickers. And yes . . . they told us how they were hired by Ricardo to kidnap you and it was his idea to demand a ransom. He was going to split the ransom with them, 50-50. Ricardo is now in custody. He has confessed to everything and is awaiting trial. When I spoke with Ricardo and expressed my anger and disappointment, he was filled with remorse and began to weep bitterly. I believe he sincerely regrets his actions and the damage he did to you, the indigenous, his family, and my administration."

"This is great news, Miguel." I said, "What will become of Ricardo?" "I would imagine he will receive a sentence of at least 5 years, Benjamin. Obviously, he will never be allowed to work for the government again. His wife and 3 small children will be the ones who will suffer financially. Ricardo's salary was the only income the family had."

"I will take care of them, Miguel." I declared, "If you tell me what Ricardo's salary was, I will send the family a monthly check." "Do you really mean that, Benjamin?" asked the astonished president. "Yes . . . I'm quite sincere, Miguel." I replied. "Benjamin . . . never in my life have I witnessed such beautiful compassion . . . such authentic love!" "Little more than a month ago, Miguel, I wouldn't have cared if Ricardo was given a life sentence and his family ended up homeless and living on the street. But after being rescued and protected by the poor; after being healed and transformed by their goodness and faith; after having my heart opened and renewed by the unspeakable beauty of the Montes Azules Biosphere Reserve . . . I am no longer the same man. Now, I see everything and everyone in the light of God's love!"

"I'm very happy for you, Benjamin." said Miguel, "It sounds like you have a brighter future awaiting you; one with a great deal more peace and joy than you ever could have imagined! If there is ever anything I can do for you, Benjamin, please let me know." "Miguel," I began, "there is something I would like to place before you for your consideration. If you think this proposal has merit and you feel moved to give it your approval, I will get started immediately." "Of course, Benjamin, please continue . . . what's in your heart?" replied the president.

"I want to move to San Cristobal so I can help the poor people who helped me. I want to spend the rest of my life and all of my wealth assisting the indigenous communities through education and medical facilities. I would like to set up a special University that would address these needs. The university would have a medical school with a hospital, a law school, a business school, various academic departments . . . such as history and theology, and a special institute for archeology and anthropology. The university system would also contain a number of elementary and secondary schools . . . some of which would be located in the jungle where they are most needed. The network of medical facilities would also sponsor and establish clinics deep within the Lacandon. I will cover all of the expenses involved. The name of the institution will be . . . *The University of the Civilization of Love.*"

"Benjamin," began Miguel, "what you have just proposed is exactly what I was hoping would take place in Chiapas some day! This whole incident, the attempted kidnapping, etc., . . . has left me very concerned about the poor people of Chiapas. Yes . . . ever since you made it clear that the indigenous were the heroes in the story, tourism in the region has risen to unheard of levels! Nevertheless, the need there is so great no amount of tourism would bring the people to where they have a right to be; but the plan you have just spelled out *would* bring them there! Yes, Benjamin, do it! Do it as soon as you can! I will give you the land and whatever legal status you and your team need or desire. Thank you, Benjamin . . . I thank you *con todo mi corazón!*" (with all my heart) "It will be my pleasure, Miguel!" I exclaimed, "I'll get started today! Adios!"

Having ridden just recently in a burro drawn cart, zipping around in a jet black, Corvette Stingray was quite an experience! I was in Manhattan in record time and I parked the car in the garage near my apartment . . . which was only 2 and a half blocks from the Plaza Hotel. As I walked along, I was approached by 3 homeless men who appeared to be more or less my age. They were dressed like The Three Stooges; each wore a black suit, white shirt and black bow tie. It was obvious, however, that they had gotten their clothes from the Salvation Army because none of the suits fit right, and they were clearly very used. The fellow playing Moe had his black hair combed straight down onto his forehead to form Moe's signature bangs. Curly was chubby and sported a shaved head. And Larry had his hair long and frizzed-out like the original character. Moe was wearing slippers, Larry had on a pair of flip-flops, and Curly wore an old pair of high, leather work boots without laces.

Hoping for a donation, they were just about to begin a comic skit when, for some strange reason, I stopped them: "Hey," I began, "have you guys had lunch yet?" "No." they replied . . . looking rather stunned. "Good!" I said, "Why don't you come with me; I'd like to treat you to lunch." "Thank you, sir . . . where are you going?" Moe asked. "The Palm Court in The Plaza Hotel . . . Afternoon Tea!" I responded nonchalantly. "Why of course . . . Afternoon Tea at The Palm Court! Where else would we be going!" chimed in Larry with a chuckle.

"Hey, wait a minute . . . aren't you Benjamin Lake; the guy who went missing in Mexico?" asked Moe. "Yes, I'm Benjamin Lake; and who are you?" "I'm Dr. Steven Rogers, cardiologist . . . I lost my position a year ago during a hostile takeover of the group I was with. I've been living on the streets ever since." "And what about you, Larry?" I asked. "I'm a corporate lawyer. My real name is Anthony Romano. I made a really stupid move politically around 8 months ago. I was fired . . . and blackballed. Now my home is an empty refrigerator carton in a remote corner of Central Park." "Curly . . . what about you?" I asked. My name is Frank McManus. I was in debt to the IRS and tried to get out by playing the stock market; I lost big time! I have a PhD in engineering from MIT and have been homeless for 2 months."

"How would you guys like a job working with me?" I asked. "You're a banker, aren't you?" said Moe, "What do we know about banking?" "Hopefully, nothing!" I replied, "I'm no longer in banking; I'm moving in a whole new direction now." "And what would that be?" asked Larry. "I'm building a new civilization!" I exclaimed. "Great! I'm a builder!" responded Curley with glee, "I've never built a civilization, but hey, there's always a first time!" "Sounds like a major undertaking, Mr. Lake. Do you think we're qualified?" asked Moe. "You're *overqualified!*" was my reply, "Your recent experiences have been the perfect formation for this special work. Now . . . we are almost at the hotel; order whatever you want. But I can highly recommend the *Parisian Ham, Gruyere Cheese and Bavarian Mustard on Pretzel Ficelle.* And for desert . . . the *Mandarin Pain Epice Tart with Gingerbread Marshmallow.* As for the choice of Tea . . . I'm partial to *The Des Amants.*"

"Good afternoon, Mr. Lake!" exclaimed the maître d' at the reservation station near the entrance to The Palm Court, "What a pleasure to see you . . . welcome home!" "Thank you Ron . . . good to see you." I replied, "You have my reservation for three?" "Let's see . . . yes, here it is." replied the maître d', all the while peering over my shoulder at The Three Stooges who were standing behind me. They appeared to be nervous and uncomfortable . . . it was all too obvious they were street people.

"Ron . . . one more thing, I will need another table near mine for these three gentlemen . . . they are my guests." I said, as I gestured in the direction of The Three Stooges. "Those three are with you?" asked the perplexed maître d'.

"Yes . . . they are my new business partners!" I replied, happily. The maître d' drew me a bit to the side and whispered: "Mr. Lake . . . those men are homeless and they stink! They may have lice . . . or even fleas!" "Ron, relax! You worry too much! I assure you, everything will be fine! Now please . . . show us our tables." "Ron took a deep breath . . . then gave a big smile: "You got it, Mr. Lake . . . right this way."

All eyes were on me and my rather striking entourage as we processed through The Palm Court. The Three Stooges held their heads high, as though they were royalty . . . while they brushed past Manhattan's high society. They were so proud to be seen in public with the famous Benjamin Lake and to be his chosen associates in the building of some mysterious, new civilization.

We no sooner were seated at our respective tables and had just begun to study the menu when I spotted Geoff and Clare parading through the restaurant. Both of them did a double take as they passed The Three Stooge's table. The first thing out of Geoff's mouth after he and his mother were seated was: "What's this all about?" he said, pointing discreetly at the stooge's table, "How the hell did they get in here?" "They're with me, Geoffrey," I replied, calmly, "They're my guests!"

"Your guests?" exclaimed a shocked Clare. "Well, actually . . . they're more than just guests; they're my new partners!" I replied with a smile. "Your new partners . . . what's this all about, Benjamin? Why did you ask to meet with me here? Was it just to introduce me to these three morons?" Geoff said as he turned around to face the stooge's table . . . at which point Curly smiled and, fluttering the fingers of his right hand, gave Geoff a comical, little wave; Moe glared at him with a grave expression on his face and gave him a military salute, while Larry, radiating a mischievous, angelic grin, held up a plate behind Moe's head . . . as if it was a halo! Geoff, donning an angry scowl, immediately turned away in a huff.

"Your friends are very talented," offered Clare, sarcastically, "I'm sure you'll go very far with them!" "I'm sure I will, Clare . . . quite far, indeed! Mexico . . . to begin with!" I countered. "Now . . . to the reason for this meeting, Geoff. I need to be free for my new mission, which is to serve the poor people who saved my life. Therefore . . . I want to pass on ownership of the bank to you. That's right, I'm giving you the bank. What do you think?"

"What do I think?" responded Geoffrey, "Rather than ask me what I think, Benjamin, you should be in a shrink's office asking him what he thinks about your thinking!" "I'm fine, Geoff. Now . . . do you want the bank or not. If not, I'll give it to the three gentlemen sitting at the table behind you; they probably deserve it more than you do anyway!"

"Ok, Benjamin . . . let's slow down here; I can see that you are serious." began Geoff. "Yes, of course I want the bank. But my concern is that you are not in your right mind and a month from now, when you come to your senses, you will have me in court saying that I took advantage of your debilitated, mental state. You may have PTSD . . . or some weird form of *The Stockholm Syndrome*." "Geoff," I countered, "you don't get PTSD from living with peaceful Franciscans and gentle Mayan orphans. And as for The Stockholm Syndrome . . . you can only develop that if you're kidnapped. I wasn't kidnapped, Geoff!"

"But there must be something wrong with you, Benjamin; who gives away a bank?" pleaded Clare. "A person worth 75 billion dollars who has decided to love and serve the poor, full-time . . . that's who!" I replied with emotion. "But Benjamin . . . you can serve humanity as a powerful banker. Remember how J. P. Morgan rescued the nation when he helped President Grover Cleveland save the US economy in the wake of the Panic of 1893." "Yes, of course I remember how that rascal's plan bailed out the country during a time of great crisis. I also remember how he made millions on the deal!" "But Benjamin," replied Geoff, "Business is a good thing . . . it's the American way! Remember what President Calvin Coolidge said in 1925: *The chief business of the American people is business!*"

"I do remember what Coolidge said, Geoff. And just 4 years later, the whole world, not just the USA, was brutalized by *The Great Depression*! So much for the worship of business! Business, Geoff, should *never* be the chief concern of any people . . . least of all a people with the degree of freedom and prosperity that Americans enjoy. "If not business, then what, Benjamin? What should people's chief concern be?" asked Geoff.

"LOVE! Geoffrey." I exclaimed, "Love should be the chief concern of people! Look at what Jesus, the master of our souls, taught: *Seek first his kingship over you, his way of holiness; and all these things will be given you besides!* (Matthew 6:33-34). We have been living a 'half-life', Geoff. Sure, we enjoy great comfort and security . . . but it still falls far short of the *abundant life* our Heavenly Father wishes to bestow upon us. Our Father knows much more about our human life than we do. We think that life is about *having*; our Father knows all too well that life is really about *giving*!

"That's why Jesus taught us to . . . *Give, and it shall be given unto you; good measure, pressed down, shaken together and running over shall men give into your bosom. For the measure you use to give, shall be measured back to you* (Luke 6:38). I have chosen to live in my Father's gifts! I have decided to embrace the abundant life! Is that really so difficult to understand, Geoff? I hope not! Now, Geoff . . . I'm a busy man; do you, or do you not want the bank?" "Yes, Benjamin," replied Geoffrey, his mother nodding her head in affirmation, "I do want the bank, and I thank you very much for this truly wonderful gift! But, out of respect for full-disclosure, I should add that I don't completely comprehend this new direction you are taking; and yet, somehow . . . I am beginning to understand it."

"Benjamin," began Clare, "What exactly are you planning to do in Mexico? How will you help the poor? Are you planning to set up a foundation?" "Great question, Clare. I will not be setting up a charitable foundation. When people establish foundations they generally say they need the foundation so that the charitable work can be sustained over time; but it has always appeared to me that the real reason for a foundation is to insure that the benefactor's wealth will be sustained over time! In most foundations, the wealthy philanthropist actually ends up giving relatively little."

"Then what type of financial plan will you use, Benjamin?" questioned Geoff. "The financial plan I'm going to use, Geoff, is called . . . *giving from the heart!* I will simply use my own money to fund all of our services. The poor need help now! They can't wait until it's convenient for me. While I'm calculating my gain . . . the poor, our brothers and sisters, will be suffering and dying! Clare . . . you asked about a foundation. While a foundation is not part of the plan, what *is* part of the plan is so much greater than any foundation could ever be; we are going to plant the seeds for a new civilization . . . *The Civilization of Love!"*

"This sounds like youthful idealism . . . a dream whose ultimate destiny is complete failure!" complained Clare. "It's not a dream and it can't fail." I responded, "And besides, Clare . . . don't be so hard on youthful idealism; young people are gifted and are capable of great things!" "But if you use your own money without replenishing it in some way . . . you will soon run out of money!" said Clare. "That's a built in risk when you give until it hurts, Clare." I replied, "But that's what authentic love requires; it's a work of the heart . . . or it's nothing at all! That's why, despite appearances to the contrary, true love never fails! When Jesus saved us by dying on the cross, it looked like the very definition of failure.

"But in all truth, Clare," I continued, "the likelihood of running out of money is practically nil; Jesus blesses our charitable giving when it flows from the heart. Recall the story of the loaves and fishes. Jesus told his disciples to give the people something to eat and the disciples replied that they only had a few loaves and a few fish . . . barely enough for themselves and Jesus. And what did Jesus do? He blessed the loaves and fishes and told the disciples to serve the people first and give them all the loaves and fishes. And what happened? Thousands of people ate and there was much more food left over than the small amount they actually began with! God blesses love, Clare!

"Jesus was teaching his disciples, and us, not to *worry about what you are to eat* (Matthew 6:25), because to love is more important . . . *Man does not live on bread alone* (Matthew 4:4). Again, when Jesus was at the well evangelizing the Samaritan woman and his disciples finally returned and asked him to eat some food . . . he told them: *I have food you know not of* (John 4:32). Loving and serving others was his food! When my father named his bank, *Praetergressus Bank*, which means, *Advance Beyond Bank* . . . perhaps it was the manifestation of a deep intuition that one day man would move *Beyond* saving and accumulating, into the higher realm of giving and sharing!

"The truth is, Clare . . . you're not really concerned about me and the possibility that I could end up penniless; in the wake of having just received a gift of astonishing value, you're concerned that I might not have anything left to share with you and Geoff; and that people might think less of me, and consequently . . . less of both of you as well, for 'squandering' the Lake fortune in such an irresponsible way. These concerns are very human, and I understand them. At the same time, I recognize that they are also trivial and self-centered . . . if one takes into consideration the bigger picture. And that's what this is all about . . . the bigger picture. You and I will always have more than enough; but there are so many of our brothers and sisters out there who have nothing. This is intolerable, and it has to change."

"And you actually think you can change that, Benjamin?" asked Geoff. "I know this much, Geoff; the only way it will ever change is if human hearts change first. It all begins in the human heart; when hearts change . . . the world will change also. That's why I said that The Civilization of Love is all about the transformation of the human heart; it will take nothing less than that to heal the world. If you imagine that politics is the answer, remember this; politics is simply a reflection of what is in the heart of man. If the heart of man is transformed in love . . . the political realm will reflect that love. It all begins in the heart."

"Well, Benjamin," began Geoff, "This has been perhaps the most fascinating discussion I've ever had. Also, this day at the Palm Court for Afternoon Tea will stand out in my memory as one of the most memorable days of my life; the day my cousin Benjamin gifted me with ownership of *Praetergressus Bank*! But I really should be going now Benjamin." "Of course, Geoff. I will tell Memphis to get everything ready for the transfer. Once I sign the papers the bank will be yours."

CHAPTER TWENTY ONE

"Gentlemen... this will be your home for the next few days." I said. "Wow! This is quite a fancy place!" exclaimed Moe. "This is just the outside." I replied, "Wait until you see the actual apartment!" We took the elevator up to my 6th floor, 4 bedroom, luxury apartment.

"OK, friends . . . here we are. Let me show each of you to your bedroom. Each bedroom has its own bathroom, complete with a Jacuzzi; and there's a roll-out bed in each bedroom closet. The refrigerator and cabinets have been filled with food, and Memphis will be here any minute with a representative from Brooks Brothers to measure each of you for a new wardrobe. Memphis has already checked you out to see that you are who you say you are.

"Now, each of you has told me you have families with whom you want to reconnect - wives and children you left out of feelings of dejection and worthlessness. Go get them - rebuild your families as you rebuild your lives. Let them know that you have been hired by Benjamin Lake to assist in the development of a network of charitable institutions in San Cristobal de Las Casas, Mexico.

"Tell your wives and children they can use my limo to come into Manhattan and they can stay here at the apartment, or at The Plaza Hotel . . . at my expense. We

will be leaving for Mexico in 7 days. I would like each of
you to move to San Cristobal with your family . . . but
that's your call. If your families want to come later . . .
that's fine, too. We will be using my private jet. Each of
you will have a simple, comfortable house, a decent salary
and a challenging but rewarding position. Dr. Steve . . .
you will direct the hospital and the Medical School.
Anthony . . . you will direct the Law School. Frank . . . you
will supervise the construction of the entire complex. Fr.
Bill, whom you will meet soon, will be, I hope . . . our
Chaplain and Spiritual Director.

"Your wives will probably want to know exactly how
much you will be making. I will be giving each of you
50,000.00 US dollars a year. That's a small fortune in
Mexico; keep in mind the exchange rate . . . 11 Pesos to one
US dollar. Plus, your room and board, your vehicle . . . as
well as health insurance for your whole family, will be
covered. This project is not about getting rich . . . this is a
mission to help our brothers and sisters who are suffering
and whose rights and dignity have been seriously
compromised. Jesus said . . . *I have come to serve and not
to be served* (Matthew 20:28). If you really want to get
rich, then it would probably be best for you to stay here in
New York and see what opportunities come your way.

"OK guys . . . I'm going to head back out to the
Hamptons. Call me or Memphis if you have any questions;
and feel free to eat at the Plaza anytime you want . . . I've
already put you on my tab. Memphis, who by the way will
also be moving to San Cristobal, will be giving each of you
$1,000.00 cash to cover any expenses you may have prior
to our trip. Thank you for joining my team . . . God bless
you!"

The next day, back at Serenitatem, I began to work on

my *"Things to Do"* list; at the top of which was a phone call to Fr. Bill . . . followed by a call to Miguel Uribe. "Hello, Fr. Bill . . . how are you!" "Fantastic, Benjamin; what's going on with you?" replied Fr. Bill. "I've looked into my heart, Fr. Bill, and I've discovered what it is I'm being called to do: I'm going to return to San Cristobal and establish a free hospital and a free school system for the poor indigenous. The project has already received the blessing of Miguel Uribe . . . President of Mexico. My team will consist of 8 adults and 7 children and we will need a place to stay while our homes are being built; can you think of some place that would be suitable for us?" I asked. "Absolutely!" replied Fr. Bill, "Do you remember that building in the far corner of the orphanage property? Well that's an 8 bedroom convent, and it was vacated about 2 months before you arrived on our doorstep. You can stay there . . . it will be perfect!"

"Wonderful, Father, just wonderful!" I exclaimed, "We can attend daily mass with you, and the children can become friends with the orphans! Also, Father, I would love it if you could be the Chaplain for the new hospital and school system." "I would be honored, Benjamin, thank you." replied Fr. Bill. "Benjamin, you said that you spoke with Miguel Uribe, so I guess you know that the trafficker's house was raided." "Yes . . . he told me all about it." I answered. "Well something amazing happened that day, and I'm quite sure no one knows anything about it except me. During the raid, the thug with the long hair, the one you tried to evangelize as you were sneaking out of town, was shot and seriously wounded. I ran down to the scene when I heard all the shooting and was allowed to minister to the dying man. I said: "My brother, what is your name?" and he answered, "Gregorio." "My name is

Fr. Bill . . . I would like to bless you and pray with you. Would that be OK, Gregorio?"

"Yes, yes, Padre!" responded the dying man, "please . . . bless me and pray with me! Help me, Padre; I want to confess." "After finishing his confession, I gave him viaticum. Then he looked into my eyes and with the most serene expression on his face, he muttered the following words: "The good friar's prayer was answered! The Lord has helped me to find the thing that was truly the most valuable . . . faith; I have my faith back, Padre! Thank you!" "And with those words on his lips, he closed his eyes and, I'm sure . . . went straight to heaven!"

"Fr. Bill . . . I'm overcome with emotion," I said . . . tears streaming down my face, "Thank you so much for racing over there and reaching out to the 'prodigal son' and helping him to return to the house of his Father." "Benjamin . . . *you* were the one who really reached out to him!" exclaimed Fr. Bill. "I never would have been able to do it had God not rescued me from my own self-destructive path. Thank you for sharing that story with me, Fr. Bill . . . I will never forget it." I said, humbled and deeply moved. "You know, Benjamin, I think your charitable project now has yet another great benefactor in heaven . . . his name is Gregorio!"

The story of Gregorio's return to the faith confirmed for me the subject matter I wanted to discuss with Miguel Uribe. "Good morning, Miguel." "Well! ¡Buenos dias, Benjamin! How are you? What can I do for you?" "We are almost ready to begin in San Cristobal," I said, "but there is something I want to run by you." "Of course, Benjamin," replied the kindly president, "what's on your mind?" "Miguel," I began, "would it be possible for you to grant Ricardo Villanueva a presidential pardon so that he could work with me? I feel that he deserves a second chance and I would like to name him Director of an Institute for Environmental Studies we are hoping to establish. He and his family would live with my team, pray with us, and work with us. Maybe he could be on probation for 5 years or so. Think about it, Miguel . . . he would be helping the very people he was so completely indifferent to."

"Wow, Benjamin . . . that's a very interesting idea! It's extremely noble of you to not only intercede on Ricardo's behalf, but also to help him reform and reestablish himself," said Miguel. "You know, Benjamin, the scandal Ricardo produced, from a political point of view, is very similar to the scandal given in your country when it was discovered that the CIA had colluded with the mafia in a failed plan to assassinate Castro. Obviously, there are differences, but they were both serious violations of the trust people place in their government. Politics aside, Benjamin, my real question is this: would the indigenous people accept Ricardo and approve of his getting off so easy?" "I think they would, Miguel; especially when they see him helping with a project that is going to improve their lives dramatically. And when they see that I have forgiven him from the heart . . . they will not hesitate to forgive him." "They're such good, humble people, Benjamin . . . I think you're right." declared the president, "Let's do it! I'll get started on the pardon immediately. Ricardo's wife and children will be the happiest people on the planet! God bless you, Benjamin Lake . . . Adios!"

Later that afternoon, I received a startling call from Memphis: "Mr. Lake . . . there are some things going on that you really need to know about." "Sure, Memphis . . . what's going on?" I replied. "Geoffrey gave a press conference this morning announcing the transfer of ownership of the bank. He told the press about your plans to move to Mexico and to work with the poor. Now . . . everyone in the known universe wants to interview you! I've received calls and requests from all the major morning shows, the late night shows, PBS, cable news, BBC, 60 minutes . . . on, and on, and on! The mayor called and suggested you do a press conference."

"Thank you, Memphis, I get the picture. If I give interviews to all the news outlets, they'll say I'm only looking for attention; and if I stay away from all of them, they'll say I'm hiding something. Therefore; I'll prepare a statement, email it to you, and you can release it to the press. I think it would be good, however, to do one interview. BBC is the most international of the bunch; so why don't you call BBC and tell them to send their US correspondent, Linda Kelly, along with a camera crew out to Serenitatem tomorrow morning at 11am. Tell them that after the interview they are welcome to join me for lunch; we can have a Bar-B-Q out on the oceanfront deck. Thanks again, Memphis . . . Ciao!"

CHAPTER TWENTY TWO

"Dr. Lake," began **Linda Kelly,** "you are one of the wealthiest people in the world, with a net worth of 75 billion dollars; why have you given away your bank and why are you moving to San Cristobal, Mexico, to serve the poor indigenous people who live there? Most people are astounded by your decision and feel you are making a big mistake. What would you say to them?"

"Just a couple of months ago," I began, "I would have agreed with them whole heartedly! But after having come to know the poor personally, and after having experienced their goodness, faith and love . . . I no longer see *anything* the same! I have come to see them as my very own brothers and sisters . . . I truly feel responsible for them. I can no longer pacify my conscience by imagining that someone else will help them . . . a government agency, for example. I now realize that I, personally, must help them: *To whom much is given, much is expected* (Luke 12:48).

"We understand that you will be using your own money to directly fund all of the charitable works you envision. Aren't you concerned that you will eventually run out of money?"

"No, Linda," I replied, "In all honesty, the thought never entered my mind until people started to bring it up. Jesus encourages heartfelt charity because he knows that the giver will discover an even greater treasure: *He who loses himself for my sake will find himself* (Matthew 16:25). And so, someone might ask, what is 'heartfelt charity'? Jesus gave us a wonderful description in the story about the charitable widow's temple donation: *The rich have contributed from their surplus wealth, but she, in her poverty, has contributed all she had . . . her whole livelihood!*

"It may seem to many people, Linda, that this type of charity is extremely difficult . . . virtually impossible! But, the truth is . . . it is much more stressful to hoard, manage, and protect wealth than it is to simply share it!"

"Dr. Lake," asked Linda, "do you plan to give up your former lifestyle; cruising in your yacht to the French Riviera, lavish parties, opulent living conditions, etc., . . .? And if so . . . don't you think you will miss all those things?"

"Yes, Linda, there will be a sea change in my lifestyle." I answered. "But the reason will not be financial. The truth is . . . those things no longer interest me; love transforms from the inside out! My awareness of the sufferings of the poor is so vivid in my heart that I could never return to the wasteful and selfish lifestyle on which I used to pride myself. I want my concern for them to be authenticated by my own lifestyle; that is . . . I would like to live in solidarity with them. My only desire now is to serve those to whom I have been sent . . . that is my joy!"

"Do you think other wealthy people should do what you are doing?" asked Linda.

"As it is, Linda . . . I'm so consumed with what I am doing that I don't have the time or energy to think about what others should or should not be doing. I do wish, however, that others could experience the liberation and joy I'm experiencing. But whether anyone should follow directly in my footsteps . . . that's between the individual and God; I would never presume to be anyone's judge in this matter. But, having said that, it's clear to me that many, many lifestyles must change if the problem of global poverty is to finally be resolved . . . and if our beautiful planet is to be rescued from the disastrous trajectory it is now on. The solution to these problems, because of their very nature, will have to be communal.

"You do, however, realize, Dr. Lake," continued Linda, "that you are providing a powerful, inspirational example for others to follow."

"Actually, Linda . . . I was *not* aware of that; I was thinking that most people would pay no attention to me. As I said; I'm focused on my mission . . . and that's more than enough for me! Nevertheless, if God chooses to use my work to inspire others . . . that would be wonderful!"

"Dr. Lake," asked Linda, "what would you say to someone who was inspired to follow your example?"

I guess I would tell them . . . when you give, give in such a way that it actually affects how you live. So many good people give, but their giving is calculated and much too measured; and so, there is really no discernable change in the way they live. Sharing is a lifestyle . . . Love is a way of life!"

"And finally, Dr. Lake," began Linda, "If someone were to ask . . . '*Are you trying to change the world?*' What would be your answer?"

"I would say that I'm just trying to love as Jesus loves; serve as Jesus serves; and forgive as Jesus forgives. Could that change the world? I don't know . . . but it could very well change hearts. And when hearts change . . . the world changes."

A few days after the BBC interview, my team and I flew to San Cristobal de Las Casas, Mexico. We began to work, and in a relatively short time we developed a very effective system of free services for people who had been excluded and forgotten for hundreds of years. I turned my 200-foot yacht, Amigo, into a hospital vessel that specialized in ophthalmology. My jet was used to transfer patients to whatever hospital they needed to go for specialized care. I sold off all of my properties . . . the Hamptons, Fifth Avenue and Costa del Sol . . . bought land and built houses for the poor.

My friend, the archeologist, Dr. Julian Ross, signed on to the project immediately. He started a very popular Archeology/Anthropology Department at the new university. One of the main reasons for the department's success was directly attributable to his talented assistants: Pakal . . . the most intelligent spider monkey to ever come forth from the Lacandon . . . and Lakamha . . . the loquacious Scarlet Macaw from Palenque!

Esperanza became the director of a special school for training ESL teachers. Her daughter, Rosario, rose to be the Chair of the new university's History department, while working on her doctoral thesis and doing extensive historical research into the life of Bartolomé de Las Casas. For my part . . . I was only too happy to teach Greek and Roman Literature.

The Three Stooges and I became Lay Dominicans. Even 'The Magnate' and Ricardo joined the Lay Dominicans. The orphan, Antonio, went on to graduate *summa cum Laude* from the new medical school. He quickly became a renowned internist and the best diagnostician in all of Mexico. Tavito, the boy bitten by the snake, went on to become a missionary priest and specialized in visiting the most remote villages.

As our friendship grew, my relationship with Rosario blossomed. As the Roman poet, Ovid said: *Love will enter cloaked in friendship's name.* We were married in the Chapel of San Nicolas by Fr. Bill, with Julian as my best man. Shortly thereafter, we were blessed with 2 sets of twins . . . 2 boys and 2 girls. "The Magnate" used his special powers to attract Memphis, and they were also married in the Chapel of San Nicholas, with me as Best man . . . and Pakal as ring bearer!

In time, as the BBC reporter, Linda Kelly predicted, our work won international recognition and similar projects sprang up all over the world. I was even awarded the Nobel Peace Prize! But what was even more astonishing was that the Pope invited me to be one of his personal consultors, and I had the rare pleasure of speaking with him quite frequently.

Eventually, the Good Shepherd came for me. I was at prayer and I heard him say: *I was hungry and you fed me; naked and you clothed me; sick and you visited me; a stranger and you welcomed me* (Matthew 25:35-40). Then he said: *Now... come home with me!* And, as St. Paul said in 1 Corinthians 15:52... *In the twinkling of an eye...* I was in Heaven!

In the beginning, my dear reader, I said I was going to share my life's journey with you; and, as you can see . . . it really was quite a journey! And although my joy here in heaven is immeasurable, sharing my story with you has actually increased my joy! Therefore, I thank you for allowing me to rejoice with you!

Made in the USA
Columbia, SC
17 August 2018